I0547462

A LONELY HEART IN NEW YORK. A MATCHMAKER IN PARIS.

NEW EDITION
INCLUDES BOOK
CLUB QUESTIONS

a novel

Hearts & Errors

FROM THE AUTHOR OF
HIGH (A CAFFEINATED LOVE STORY)

COREY M.P.

HEARTS AND ERRORS. Copyright © 2019 by Corey M.P.
All rights reserved.

Published in the United States of America.
Published 2019.

French Press Publishing

ISBN-13: 978-0-578-44783-4

Book cover image and design by Corey Muñoz Panergo

For my sisters, Mia and Paula—I love you.
And for my dear friends, Christina and Celeste.

To Paris, it was love at first sight.

Contents

HEARTS AND ERRORS

*"We all want love. We all need love.
And no matter how much we push it away
or pretend to deny ourselves of it,
our hearts will always desire it."*

– Lana Levine (HEARTS AND ERRORS)

HEARTS AND ERRORS

1

Cursed

It all began with a blue Sharpie.

A blue Sharpie and an I'm Sorry Card.

It will be three years in twelve days since it happened, and I still get knots in my stomach whenever the date approaches.

I write a monthly column for *Trend Magazine,* a job I used to think was a dream come true. But now I'm convinced that accepting the job was a curse, because ever since I had agreed to write a column called, "Single and Loving It," I've been single but *not* loving it.

I've spent the last hour staring at the blank screen on my laptop, struggling to write an article that's due in a few days. The only thing I've been able to come up with is a page full of invisible words. I close my laptop and place it on the side table next to my bed. I drag my feet to the kitchen and grab a glass of water. I take a couple of sips and pour the rest out into the sink. After the water drains, I realize how quiet it is in my apartment. I can hear myself thinking about things I wish I could erase—like Roy, and that particular day and his blue Sharpie and the damn card.

I push the kitchen window open while an ambulance wails by. I shut my eyes, letting the noise of Manhattan filter in and distract me. The loud siren soon fades into cars honking, a dog barking, and people yelling down on the street. But none of it helps. Instead, the cold air becomes nostalgic, bringing me back to four years ago, when I met Roy. Back when I used to think the world of him.

Roy was a breath of fresh air, following the amusing batch of men I had dated before him. There was Jake the stand-up comic, who never laughed, followed by Rick, the bartender, who hated alcohol but loved his tips. Then there was David the stockbroker, whose lifelong dream was to own the most expensive penthouse on Park Avenue.

So, after meeting Roy, I thought he was different.

Roy and I met at the final luncheon at a New York Writers Conference where we were seated together. He said hello, and I said hello, and we shook hands before we even sat down. I wore a navy-blue dress with my long dark hair up in a bun. Roy looked handsome in his white Oxford shirt and gray slacks. He was average height, short blonde wavy hair, blue eyes, a body of a surfer, and a vocabulary of a genius.

We started a conversation, even before the appetizers arrived, and by the time the coffee and desserts were served, we had already exchanged phone numbers. At one point, Roy whispered in my ear and said he liked my green eyes. I whispered back and said I liked his smile.

He called me the next day, and soon, we were inseparable. And for a year, it was bliss. Until he lovingly broke my heart on Valentine's Day.

I woke up early that morning, the sun seeping through the bedroom window in my apartment in the Upper West Side. I playfully wrestled my feet underneath the flannel sheets, searching for Roy's warm and masculine legs. When I couldn't find them, I imagined he was in the kitchen making me a delicious breakfast, which he liked to do. We had planned on spending the day in bed and only stepping out for dinner at our favorite tapas place in Chelsea. But when I sat up, there was no sign of Roy. What greeted me instead was a red envelope sitting on my side table. I pushed the sheets in a hurry and reached for the envelope, expecting to see something sweet and romantic. My heart stopped when I pulled out the card from the envelope. Instead of a "Valentine's Day Card", it was an "I'm Sorry Card". Written inside with a blue Sharpie, were seven words. *I can't give you what you want.*

What he couldn't give me was a commitment. It wasn't like I was asking for marriage. All I wanted was for him to define our relationship, but he couldn't do that. A year together and he couldn't even write my name on the card. He didn't even sign it. A vocabulary of a genius, but that's all he could say.

Three years later, and I still wonder how long he had planned and plotted his escape for me not to notice him fleeing before I woke up that morning. I never heard from Roy again. He simply disappeared. I expected more from him and the relationship. I wish I had known better. But I didn't. And I was miserable. I ripped his card into a hundred pieces that day and flushed it down the toilet. I tossed my old sheets, comforters, and pillows, and bought new ones. I lugged my side table out on the sidewalk and purchased a replacement from the over-priced furniture store down the street, and made sure it didn't resemble the old table. I scoured through my apartment, removing every piece of anything that be-longed to Roy or reminded me of him. I ended up rear-ranging my furniture in the living room, to the point where it didn't make sense. My orange accent chair now sat alone in an odd space in between my bedroom and living room, but I left it there anyway because it fooled me into thinking I was fine. Moving out even crossed my mind, but I couldn't get myself to leave my cozy apart-ment.

A day later, there I was broken-hearted when I re-ceived a call from the editor of *Trend Magazine* offering me my dream job. I was ecstatic. It was the best news I had received since the breakup. Nothing else would've cheered me up. Writing for *Trend Magazine* was my dream. My knees shook, and my heart pounded as I stayed on the line, waiting to hear about my assignment. When they asked me to write a monthly column dedi-cated to single women, my heart sunk. How appropriate, I thought. With the freedom to name it, I called it "Single and Loving It." I don't know what I was thinking. This was unfamiliar territory. I was still in shock. Roy had just left me, and I needed a minute to let things sink in. But there was no time to do that. My first article was due in a week. The only option I had was to accept the chal-lenge head on and hope I could deliver my best work and somehow heal in the process.

In the midst of crying, overdosing on gelato and po-tato chips, I wrote my first column. I lied about how great it felt to be single, like I'm about to lie about how great it still feels now.

OK, maybe I wasn't always lying. By the time I wrote my fourth article, I was enjoying my freedom, and it reflected in my stories. Single women were writing to the magazine wanting more from me, and it felt rewarding. I went from feeling dejected and rejected to feeling needed. I frequented clubs and bars and hung out with my single friends, and savored every second of it. I called it research. And, well, it was. But that didn't last long. Most of my single friends are now either engaged or married or about to have their first child. They've all moved on to greater things, while I have managed to do the exact opposite.

It will be three years in two weeks since I began writing for *Trend Magazine.* I don't know how much longer I can keep this up. How do I continue writing about something I don't believe in anymore?

My phone beeps. Three missed calls and two voicemails. I hope it's not Danielle updating me about how large her breasts have become since the pregnancy or Cindy venting about how stressed out she is with her wedding plans, or else I am going to lose it. It's not that I'm not happy for them because I am. But I need to focus on writing about how much I love being single, and they're not helping.

My phone rings. It's my editor. I don't want to pick it up, but I have to.

"Hi, Craig," I answer, sitting on my couch.

"Hey, Lana." He pauses. "I'm not calling you about your deadline," he says, dragging his voice.

"Is everything OK?" I ask, my stomach tensing up.

"Listen, I need to be honest with you." He pauses again.

I don't like the sound of that.

"Lana, your column is not doing well." He sighs. "There's been a huge decline in readership the last few months and we haven't received any fan letters." He pauses for a second. "Is everything OK with you?" he asks, concerned.

"Sure, everything is OK," I lie.

"Well, something needs to change, and quick. Because whatever you've been doing lately is not working. There's no excitement. No thrill." He pauses. "Give me something good. I'd hate to cancel your column."

Craig has always been forthright, and I usually appreciate it. But I can't stand it at the moment.

I curl up on the couch, my stomach turning.

There it is. The magazine wants to break up with me, too. But this time, I'm the one who can't give them what they want.

2

The Article

After my disappointing conversation with my editor, I made an appointment to see my doctor straight away. Every time Valentine's Day approaches, the same thing happens—my stomach tenses up, and I worry about being alone. All thanks to Roy and his blue Sharpie. I know I need to get over it, but it seems impossible at the moment, especially while I'm stressing out about my column. I'm sure my doctor thinks I'm a hypochondriac. He's probably right. Last year, he told me there was nothing wrong with me. He said the same thing the year before that. I've seen him every year for the last two years, and it wasn't for my yearly check-ups.

I rush to the doctor's office despite being aware that I would be spending most of my time staring into space in the waiting room.

"Please take a seat and fill out these forms," directs the young medical assistant who glances at her cell phone conveniently located next to her keyboard. Her thick hair is up in a messy ponytail. Her scrubs are of geometric squares in teal, pink, and gray, which coincidentally matches the paint on the wall. Her crooked name tag reads: Gladys.

"Oh, I was here last year. I'm a patient of Dr. Martin," I explain, thinking maybe she thinks I was a new patient.

"Dr. Martin moved to Chicago last month. You're now seeing Dr. Arnold. You should've received a letter in the mail. Anyway, since you're a new patient to Dr. Arnold, you have to fill out these forms again," she says, and quickly checks her phone.

"OK, thanks," I say, taking the forms with me.

I proceed to a chair next to a side table with a dusty lamp surrounded by magazines.

I take the pen that's tied to the clipboard and lightly tap it on my lap as I fill out the forms.

Patient Name: Alana Levine

Address: 450 West 74th Street, #12 F, New York, NY 10023

I scan through the next few questions and realize how even medical forms have a way of reminding me I'm single.

Sex: ~~It's been a while~~ Female

Age: ~~31~~ ~~32~~ 33

I draw a blank.

I can't remember how old I am.

I know the whereabouts. Thirty-something. 32? *Maybe.* 33? 31? *I hope.*

I end up filling out my birth date while discreetly calculating my age before coming up with 34. *Darn.* I was hoping for 31.

Marital Status: Single

See what I mean?

A few more questions then I get to the Pain Screening portion.

Circle a number from 0-10 that best describes how much pain you are having now.

I want to circle 10.

I glance at the drawings below. It's the Wong-Baker FACES Pain Rating Scale. Each face has an expression and a number below. I stare at the fourth face and immediately agree. *That's my face! I'm Hurts Even More!* I circle six.

Minutes later, I hand my forms back to Gladys.

"Have a seat. We'll call you," she says, without making eye contact. She takes my forms and moves it into a slot.

I return to my seat. An old lady wearing a colorful crochet hat is staring at the dreadful fuchsia carpet, her walker positioned in front of her. I wonder how her life has been all these years. Has love been kind to her?

I lean back, resting my head on the wall behind me remembering my conversation with Craig. The thought tenses me up. What should I do? As much as quitting the column could potentially save my love life, it could also hurt my career. I need to save my love life and keep my career. But how do I do that? Is it possible to keep both?

I glance at the stack of magazines next to me. Without looking, I retrieve one and rest it on my lap. It's a travel magazine, an old one with the cover slightly ripped and faded. The headline reads, *Make a Wish*. Right below is a beautiful photo of the Trevi Fountain.

"Make a wish," I mumble to myself, lifting it up and fanning the pages.

A loose leaf falls on my shoes.

I pick it up and notice the creases across the page. I iron it out with my hand, pressing it against my leg. As I do, I find myself drawn to a pull quote that says:

I remember having this sudden urge to get lost somewhere, discover something new, or dream something big.

I hold it closer, my eyes gawking at the words. The title says: "*Merci,* Paris"

Without skipping a beat, I move down the page and start reading the article.

My mother and I traveled to Paris from California for a short sojourn in the spring of 1994. She had invited me at the last minute to accompany her to visit a close friend who had fallen ill. I almost didn't go, because I was saving my vacation days for a trip to Costa Rica in July with some friends. But in the end, I couldn't pass up an opportunity to travel with my mother—something that we rarely did. And I couldn't resist going back to Paris.

I had been to Paris a couple of times before, but never in the spring. It was as beautiful as it was when I went in the summer and in the fall.

It was on my third day in The City of Light when something unexpected and unforgettable happened—something that would change my life forever.

My mother was spending the day with her friend, and it was my first day alone since we arrived. I left our hotel and took a long relaxing stroll. I walked along the Seine River and crossed the Pont Saint-Michel and ended up at the Notre Dame Cathedral on Île de la Cité. I sat on a bench and watched the tourists clicking their cameras at the amazing structure that stood proudly before us. Later, I strolled along the Fifth Arrondissement and found myself inside the Shakespeare and Company bookstore on Rue de la Bucherie. I spent an hour on every floor before purchasing a book. I thought about heading back toward the Seine and planned on reading my book along the riverbank, but for some reason, when I exited the bookstore, I felt different. I remember having this sudden urge to get lost somewhere, discover something new, or dream something big. I guess it is one of the many reasons why Paris is such a magical city, because it has a way of calling you in, and inviting you to see things differently, to live differently, to be a different you—even for a moment. It's indescribable, and the only way you would ever understand it is if you experience it yourself.

Embracing these new feelings, I sped down the block and made a sharp turn somewhere unfamiliar. I kept going along this particular road, and when I noticed the sounds of the city slowly fading into the background, I felt this distinct sense of exuberance. It was around then that I stumbled upon a lovely café tucked in a narrow alley. Something about it draws me in. And when I entered the café, I was exhilarated. As if I had discovered something no one else had before, even though I knew it wasn't true because the place was bustling with people. When a seat opened up, I grabbed it and spent the rest of the afternoon reading and nursing my cup of coffee.

I was lost in my own little world, devouring the pages of my book, taking slow sips of my lukewarm coffee, when an old man with a kind face and a gentle smile approached me. He had silver hair, and he wore a white button-down shirt and brown trousers. He offered me his hand, and I recall closing my book in haste, taking his hand, and following him across the room, like I knew him. We stopped at a table where a man who looked like he was in his midthirties sat alone, immersed in the pages of his book. The old man leads me to the empty chair next to the stranger, and without hesitation, I sat down. Regardless of how perplexed I was by what was going on, I didn't ask any questions. I didn't want to. I was too amused by what was happening to me. My heart raced with every second that passed, and I grew nervous and excited. I glanced at the stranger who looked surprised by our arrival and seemed as confused as I. He gazed at me and we locked eyes. He said something, and I said something, and within minutes, everything became a blur. The old man disappeared in the back of the café, and soon, I was sharing a pastry with a stranger and sipping a fresh cup of coffee.

Later that day, I learned that the old man was the owner of the café. But more importantly, I learned that he was a matchmaker.

Love was at the lowest priority in my life at that time. I was in my late thirties, and I thought I had already given up on love a long time ago, especially after enduring one bad relationship after another. But on that spring day, at that café, I had a change of heart. And I owe it all to that trip to Paris.

I guess love does come when you least expect it because I wasn't looking for love. But maybe deep inside, I was. I left the café that day with my coffee mate, my love, and my soulmate.

Maybe that's why I wanted to get lost somewhere, because I wanted to be found.

The café is called Le Café Dubois. Monsieur Francois Dubois is the beloved matchmaker. It has been said that ever since his wife passed in 1993, he began matchmaking people in his café. Not too many know about this little secret. But the rumor is that more and more single people have entered alone, and have left with someone.

If you wish to visit the café, the best thing to do is start from the Shakespeare and Company bookstore on 37 Rue de la Bucherie.

When you are facing the bookstore, proceed to your left, and make a right at the end of the block. You will pass a row of souvenir shops and a couple of restaurants. Keep going. When the noise dissipates, you'll know you're getting closer. There will be a narrow alley tucked away in between the buildings. Go down this alley and follow it, as it curves left. The café sits there by itself. Don't blink, or you might miss the beautiful red frame door. Look up, and you'll see the sign that says, Le Café Dubois. The door is heavy, so push hard. When you enter, pass through the red velvet curtains, and voilà!

You have arrived.

Good luck on your journey. I hope you find exactly what it is you are looking for.
Sylvia James
Paris, France

Goosebumps fill every inch of my body as I sit on the edge of my seat.

I look up. The old lady with the walker is gone. I straighten up in my seat and stare at the article in my hand.

I fold it and slip it inside my purse.

It all makes sense now. My column isn't working, because like me, no one wants to be alone. We all want love. We all need love. And no matter how much we push it away or pretend to deny ourselves of it, our hearts will always desire it.

I dash past Gladys and tell her that I no longer need to see the doctor.

I am fine.

3

A Matchmaker in Paris

I phone Craig the second I enter my apartment.

"Craig, it's Lana," I say, eager to tell him my new discovery.

"Your deadline's coming up," he says, typing away in the background.

"I figured out why my column isn't working."

"Great. Email me your story," he says, sounding curt.

"That's it? You don't want to know why?" I say, disappointed.

"When have I ever asked you about why you write what you write? I believe in you. I know you can write. That's why we hired you. Whatever it is that you believe in, write it down and send it to me. I don't care what you do as long as you get it to me on time," Craig says, still hitting the keys on his keyboard.

He is right. He has never asked me about why I write what I write or where my inspiration comes from. But I like Craig. He has always been honest with me, and I appreciate that.

"I'll get it to you soon," I finally say.

"I need it by Monday," he says, and stops typing.

"Monday?" I repeat, hoping he'd push it further.

"Monday, the 5th," he confirms.

"Sounds good," I say, my head spinning.

I have no idea what to write.

What am I going to write?

"Lana, whatever it is that has been bothering you the last few months, let it go. It's not worth your time. Give me something good on Monday. I'd hate for us to have to cancel your column," he finishes.

That's the second time he's said that.

"Monday, it is," I say with zest.

We hang up. A second later, my phone rings. It's Danielle. I take a deep breath before answering the phone.

"Hi, Danielle," I say, feigning a cheery tone.

"Hey. I'm calling because I saw the calendar," she says.

My head drops. "Oh… that," I reply.

Whenever it hits February, Danielle knows I go through my *sick phase*. It's when anything that reminds me of Valentine's Day stresses me out, hence the stomach pains and sudden trips to the doctor.

"How are you holding up?"

"OK. I guess." I pause. "Is there a place out there where they don't celebrate Valentine's Day, so I can skip all the hearts and Eros crap?"

"Eros? Do you mean arrows?"

"No, Eros—as in Cupid."

"Eros, arrows, whatever. I'm telling you, Lana, all you need to do is go on a date," she says.

"You make it sound so easy," I say, lounging on my orange armchair, positioned right in between my living room and my bedroom.

"But you've been on dates recently, haven't you?"

"I've been on bad dates," I retort.

"Roger was nice, wasn't he?" she says.

"He was a bit too forward for me. The first thing he asked me when we sat down for dinner was my thoughts on having an open relationship. We just met." I shake my head. "Thanks, but no thanks. Please don't set me up with your neighbors anymore. Actually, don't ever set me up again. Period," I say with a tense laugh.

"He was probably nervous. Anyway, I'm sorry that didn't work out. What about speed dating?"

"I tried it, remember? I sped out of the place as soon as I realized how many creeps were out there," I say.

"That's why you have to try Matchnow.com. That's how I found my Ted."

"I know that's how you found Ted. I know that," I say, rolling my eyes.

Danielle tells everyone about how she met Ted through an online dating service. Great for them, but that's not how I want to find love.

"I'm only trying to help," she says.

Despite her insistent ways, I love Danielle. She's my best friend. She's been there for me through thick and thin, and I mean including my weight fluctuations. I was thick in college and thin after I graduated. I spent too much time with my books and my boyfriend at the time, and partied too little. She on the other hand, partied a little too much. It's amazing how she went from smoker and serious beer drinker to a completely clean and sober mother-to-be.

"I know my column is bad luck. That's why I'm date-less," I say, dragging my feet to the kitchen.

"Why do you always say that? Your column is not bad luck. You got the job *after* you and Roy broke up. It's not the other way around."

"He broke up with me," I say, correcting her.

"You know what I mean," she says.

"Yeah, I know," I say, sighing. "Listen, I love you, but I have to go. I need to write my column. The last thing I want is to get fired."

"They're not going to fire you, Lana."

"Don't be too sure. You should've heard what Craig said to me today."

"All right. Well, call my cell if you need me. I'll have it on vibrate, so we don't wake up Ted. I'm too pregnant to sleep anyway," she says, referring to her constant visits to the bathroom and her secret rendezvous with the refrigerator.

"I'm not going to call you in the middle of the night," I say, shaking my head.

"Fine. Talk soon," she says. And we hang up.

It's Friday night. I can't believe all I have is the weekend to come up with an article. I retrieve my laptop from the bed and head to the kitchen. After drinking the left-over sangria from when I hosted Cindy's bridal shower at my place, which now tasted flat, I come up with absolutely zilch.

Is this writer's block or simply writer's bad luck?

I minimize the blank Word document on my screen. Then I go online and type Matchnow.com.

I cringe.

The first thing I see is a pop-up window that reads: *Click here to find your one true love.*

I slam my laptop shut.

I can't do it.

It seems too technical and too formal for something that shouldn't be. I may be looking to find someone, but this is not how I would like to meet him. I guess I'm too much of a hopeless romantic—in love with the idea of being swept away. Maybe that's my problem.

I'm happy it worked out for Danielle, but online dating is not for everyone, at least not for me.

I walk to my bed and lay flat on my back, staring at another blank canvas—my ceiling.

It must have been the sangrias, because within seconds, I fall asleep. When I awake, my head feels heavy on the pillow. I force myself up, dragging my weight toward the window where I witness a beautiful orange sky. I look down on the empty streets and sidewalks. A Chinese restaurant menu blows in the wind and lands on a metal grate. I spin around and reach for my purse on the floor, digging inside for the magazine article. I stand by the dining table, unfolding it quickly and reading the pull quote quietly.

I remember having this sudden urge to get lost somewhere, discover something new, or dream something big.

I read it once more, this time, out loud. And for some reason, I see a clear vision of myself in Paris. There I am, sitting outside a café, sipping coffee with a long scarf wrapped around my neck, watching people walk by, the soft wind blowing against my skin. And in my dreamlike state, I get lost in this thought for a while, marveling at the idea.

I sit down. My eyes settle on the floor on a pile of copies of *Trend Magazine*. I glance at the article in my hand. Out of nowhere, there's a jolt inside of me, a giant push from within.

What if I go to Paris?

My heart leaps at the thought. A rush of energy fills my body. I reach for my laptop and turn it on. I take a deep breath and start typing.

A Matchmaker in Paris
My dear readers,

For three years now, we have gotten to know each other within the pages of a magazine, where I have shared many anecdotes and observations about living the single life. Through my articles, you and I have laughed together, explored Manhattan together, and even grown together. I have enjoyed your kind comments, your emails, and your thoughtful letters. I cherish these moments and value the time you have given me each month, reading my words, and listening to what I have to say.

But recently, somewhere between writing these articles and reflecting on my life, I have hit a wall. It occurred to me that even after all these years of sharing my life with you, I have managed to stay cooped up and stranded in my past. A past where I continue to dwell on an old love that has long forgotten me. And although I have enjoyed the perks of being single, I haven't embraced the concept of being alone. Deep inside my soul, I have been afraid, lonely, and miserable, and I have tried to cover up these feelings for far too long.

But now it's time to let them go.

This realization came to me recently, in a form of an irony—a magazine article, a loose page that fell on my feet at the doctor's office. When I picked up this piece of paper, I was drawn to the pull quote in the middle of the page. There it was, big and bold, screaming at me. It said: "I remember having this sudden urge to get lost somewhere, discover something new, or dream something big."

These words grabbed me, and before I knew it, I had already read the entire article. It was a beautiful story about a woman who stumbled upon a café, tucked away in an alley in Paris. A café where an old man unexpectedly approached her, took her hand, and walked her to a table across the room, where a young man sat alone. In seconds, they were introduced, and in minutes, they were inseparable. It turned out, the old man, who happened to be the café owner, was also a matchmaker.

I couldn't believe this story was real. But it happened to this lady—this lady, who at that point, had already given up on love. But somehow, when she set herself free and allowed herself to get lost— love found her.

I held the article in my hands, gripping the sides, gaping at the words. Soon, I was lost in my own world, next to a row of empty chairs in a waiting room, reflecting on my life, asking myself a question I had never bothered to ask before.

Why am I single?

Or why are we single?

Is it by choice? Or have we been bruised by a bad breakup that now we fear starting over? Are we afraid of commitment or of getting hurt? Are we single because we haven't found the right one, or the right one hasn't found us? Are we too picky? Or are we genuinely having fun being single? Do we love being single so much that now the universe believes this is how we want to live our lives and have left us alone for good?

I hope not.

I know there's nothing wrong with being single, and to some of us, it is a choice we have made, and we are truly happy.

But I am not happy.

And I have to admit I'm over it.

I'm over the empty bed in the morning, the one cup of coffee on the table, the quiet nights and predictable weekends. I'm ready to be thrilled again and be swept off my feet. I'm ready for the phone calls, the dinner plans, and the dancing. I'm ready for the butterflies in my stomach and the first kiss, the second kiss, and the thousands more to come. I'm ready for the arguments and disagreements and the resolutions that follow. I'm ready to fall in love again.

As these thoughts ran through my head, a rush of energy came over me. And I could not sit still. It was around then that "I remember having this sudden urge to get lost somewhere, discover something new, or dream something big."

At that moment, it was clear. In order to seek love again, I must leave my comfort zone. Because what if all this time I have given up on love, when love hasn't given up on me? What if all these years I have been waiting for something to happen, something to change, when that something and that change was supposed to come from me? They say love comes to those who wait. But what if waiting is the same as giving up?

Starting today, I have decided only to live and be in the present. Today I have decided to be honest with myself and with all of you. Today I will embrace fear and take a chance. Today I will change my life and move on.

As I am writing this, something in my gut is telling me I must go to Paris and search for that one café and meet the matchmaker. I know it's probably going to be a big mistake.

But what if it isn't?

Besides, when was the last time I ever took a chance at love, or at anything?

Yes, I will go to Paris.

This is my time to fly.

Here's to us and to taking risks.

All my best,

Lana Levine

I scroll up the page and read what I had written. When I finish, it feels as though a heavy load has been lifted off my shoulders.

Without hesitation, I email the article to Craig, along with a note:

Craig,

It's time I stay true to my readers and to myself. Otherwise, what's the point? If this is to be the last story I ever write for Trend Magazine, I completely understand.
Lana

An hour later, I pick up the phone and dial Danielle's number.

"Hello?" she answers.

"Did I wake you?"

"I knew you'd call. I'm in the kitchen eating leftover pizza. Have you ever had cold pizza? It's not bad," she says.

"I'm going to Paris," I blurt.

"Great. Can I go, too?" she says, while chewing.

"I'm not kidding. I'm going," I say, in a stern voice.

"Wait, what? Are you serious? It's five in the morning. You're probably dreaming. Oh no. Are you sleepwalking? Wake up, Lana!" she says, in a loud whisper.

"I'm about to pack my bags. I'm going."

"You are serious." Danielle stops chewing. "What has gotten into you? A few hours ago, you wanted to avoid anything that reminded you of Valentine's Day. But now you're going to the most romantic city in the world?"

"I read an article about a matchmaker in a café in Paris. I'm going to find him."

"Hold on. Are you joking right now? I don't know if you're serious or not."

"I'm not joking," I confirm.

"Oh, sweetie. That's what they have online dating for. Save your plane ticket money. I'm telling you, you have to try online dating," she insists.

"Enough about online dating. Besides, it's for my column," I say, lying.

I already sent my story to Craig.

"For your column," she repeats, suspiciously.

"And if love finds me there, then so be it," I finish.

"I knew it! I knew there was a *but* there somewhere," she says, trying to keep her voice down.

"Danielle, I'm going," I say, dismissing her.

"OK, OK, I get it. You're going. Fine. Go." She sighs. "I envy you and the freedom you have right now." She pauses. "I hope you know I'm always here for you, pregnant or not pregnant."

"I know you are."

"Do you promise to call me when you get to Paris?"

"I promise."

I hang up the phone, unzip my suitcase, and swing my closet door wide open.

4

All Unpacked

After hours of carefully distributing my clothes all over my bedroom floor, I manage to pack absolutely nothing. My pants are neatly folded and stacked on one side of the bed, my shoes lined up on the floor, and my toiletries organized, but my mind in complete disarray. Yes, I want to find love. But will going to Paris be the right decision? Am I kidding myself about finding love in a café I've never been to because of an article I read in a doctor's office?

I pluck myself off the floor and swerve my orange chair to face my bedroom. I sit down, staring at my belongings, pondering about my heart. Is it worth going? Is it worth the trouble? Can I find the same thing online?

Today is February second. It's only a couple of weeks away from Valentine's Day…my *favorite* holiday. I can already see all the heart-shaped candies, giant red hearts, and romantic cards filling up stores and window shops. The thought of it sickens me. I hope wherever Roy is now that he's alone, and that someone else had left him and had broken his heart. Like he had broken mine. But I don't mean it. Being hurt makes me say harsh things. I can't believe I'm still feeling this way, and it's been three years.

Three years!

Aren't I supposed to be over it by now? Danielle is certain that the only way I'll get over it is by dating again. I've tried. It didn't work. She thinks I should try harder, but how the hell does one try harder at dating? Cindy thinks I need closure in order to move on, but what kind of closure?

I get up and pace back and forth, unable to decide what to pack, maybe because I can't decide whether to go or stay.

I pick up the phone and dial Cindy's number. It goes to voicemail. She's probably running around planning her wedding, as usual. I dial Danielle's number next. It also goes to voicemail.

Hours pass and I've raided the freezer multiple times for ice cream. I toss the empty container of Ben and Jerry's Chunky Monkey ice cream in the garbage and slowly work my way back to my bedroom where my empty suitcase awaits.

What do I do now? Do I go?

I already wrote my last story and sent it to Craig, and the article says I'm going to Paris, which means I have to go. I can't lie to the few readers I have left. That wouldn't be fair unless I call Craig now and tell him not to publish it. But doing so would speed up the life of my column and probably end my writing career. But it could also be the only way to end the curse of my love life. As my thoughts confuse me, my cell phone rings. It's Danielle.

"Hey, I'm still here," I answer, sounding disappointed.

"Still here? Do you mean you're at home or you're at the airport waiting to board?"

"No, I'm still at home."

"Wow. I didn't expect that. You sounded so determined this morning. I thought you had already left for sure."

"Yeah, well…" I say, dragging my voice.

"Did you change your mind?"

"Not exactly. More like I can't make up my mind. I keep wondering if it's even worth going. Will this matchmaker be the answer to everything? I mean, what if I don't find what I'm looking for?"

"That's the risk you take, Lana. Online or not online. You don't know what you're going to find. I didn't know what I was going to find when I signed up for the dating website, but I tried anyway, and it ended up being worth it."

"Yeah, you're right. It's a risk." I say, losing the courage to go. Like I'm not ready to take that risk, but why?

Am I afraid of moving on?

"Well, at the end of the day, it's your decision. All I can say is follow your heart," she says.

"Follow my heart," I repeat lifelessly, while the other line enters.

"You have another call," she says, interrupting my sour mood.

"Yup, I know. It's probably Cindy calling me back," I say, slouching on the bed.

"Aren't you going to answer it? Should I hold on?"

"Sure, hang on." I switch to the other line without checking the caller ID.

"Hello," I answer, turning my head toward the window.

"Hey, Al."

My eyes widen.

Only one person has ever called me Al. And it's not Cindy.

5

Blast from the Past

Roy?

Oh my god.

I sit up.

What do I do? Do I hang up? Why is he calling? Why is he calling me now? Why is he calling me at all?

"Y-yes?" I reply, doing my best to sound calm while holding my breath. My hands are shaking. I grip the phone harder trying not to drop it.

"It's Roy," he says.

Yes, I know who it is.

What do I do about Danielle who's still on hold?

I inhale slowly.

"Oh, hi. Can you hold on? I have someone on the other line," I say, trying to disguise my heart pounding off my chest.

"Sure," he says.

I click back to Danielle.

"Danielle?"

"Yes, I'm still here."

"You will not believe this. Roy is on the other line. He's on the other line!" I say, now standing on the bed.

"What! Roy? Hang up on him!" she says, slamming the refrigerator door.

"Too late, I already told him to hold on. What do I do? What do I say?" I sit back on the bed, trying to hold myself together.

"First of all, calm down. And just… just… Oh, I don't know, Lana. Tell him how you've been feeling all these years. How much he's hurt you. Tell him he's an asshole," she says, in an angry tone.

"All these years? I don't think I want him to know that. He might think I'm still in love with him, when I am absolutely not. I swear I'm not," I say.

"Well, then, tell him you haven't forgiven him or something," she says.

"I'll figure it out. I'll call you back. Thanks," I say, rushing her off the phone.

"Good luck!" she finishes.

I switch back to the other line with no clue of what to say or do.

"Roy?" I utter.

"Al, how are you?" he asks, his voice a little shaky.

I don't know what to make of that question? I want to scream on the phone and say 'how the hell do you think?' but I don't want him to know I'm still hurting.

"I'm great. How are you?" I reply, lying.

"I'm good." He pauses. "It's been a long time since we've talked."

Of course, it's been a long time. You left me three years ago.

"Yes, it has." I say, grinding my teeth.

"Listen, I know you're probably asking yourself why I'm calling."

"Why are you calling?" I ask.

"Well, it's just that I've been thinking about you a lot lately," he says, sounding relieved after the words leave his mouth.

"You have?" I ask, surprised.

"Yes, I have. And I was hoping we could speak in person. There's a lot I need to say to you."

"Don't you think it's a little late for that?" I ask, wondering why he picked now to do this.

"I was hoping it wasn't." He clears his throat. "I made a mistake three years ago, and trust me, I'm not trying to make up for it. I-I just really want to explain a few things to you. That's all."

"Well, you can do it over the phone," I reply sternly, while my heart slowly softens.

What is happening to me? Don't I hate this guy?

He chuckles uncomfortably. "I get it. You're probably with someone else and I'm an idiot for reaching out to you."

No, I'm not with anyone else, but yes, you are an idiot.

"What do you want me to say, Roy? You left like I didn't even matter. And it hurt for a while, but I'm over it."

I'm obviously not.

"Can I come over?" he blatantly asks.

Is he kidding? Why is he still insisting?

"No. You can't come over," I reply, with a dry laugh.

"Right, because you're with someone else now. Was that him on the other line?" he says, digging for information.

"What do you want, Roy?" I ask, now agitated.

"I want to see you. I want to talk," he explains.

Within seconds of contemplation, I do the unexpected. As though I have no choice.

"I can meet you at the café across the street, but you're not coming over," I say, in the nicest tone possible.

"I'll be there in 10 minutes," he says, his voice no longer shaking.

Ten minutes? Where the hell is he?

"O-K. I-I guess I'll see you in ten minutes," I say, wondering if all this is actually happening.

I hang up the phone and rush to the bathroom and splash cold water on my face.

Why am I going to see Roy?

I find an outfit straight away with the help of my unpacked clothes spread throughout my room like a department store display. I change to a pair of jeans and a cream sweater. I peek out the window. I can see the café from my apartment.

I can't believe I'm doing this.

Why am I doing this?

I pick up the phone and ring Danielle.

"What happened?" she answers, after half a ring.

"I'm meeting him at the café across the street," I blurt, knowing full well that she would disagree.

"Are you crazy? Lana, why in the world would you do that?"

"He wanted to come over and explain himself. Going across the street is our compromise."

She lets out a long sigh and surrenders. "Whatever. Fine. But be strong. No matter what, don't fall for his bullshit," she demands.

"I won't. I know better now."

"I know you do." She sighs. "Well, I want to hear all about it. Call me when it's over."

"I will. Of course, I will."

I look out the window again and see Roy. My heart beats faster.

"I have to go."

"OK. Be strong. Bye."

I hang up the phone and release the curtains.

It's show time.

6

It's Only Coffee, Right?

Why did I agree to meet him right now, or at all?

He doesn't deserve to see me. But maybe it's not about him deserving to see me, but more about him owing me an explanation.

My legs and feet hesitate with every step as I make my way to the café. My heart is pounding, while a barrage of emotions comes over me. I already know this is all a mistake.

I struggle to take the last few steps before I hit the open door. I catch a glimpse of Roy sitting by the window with a cup of coffee in his hand, gazing out. He doesn't see me yet. He looks different. His head is shaved. The thick gold locks I used to run my fingers through are gone.

I manage to make it inside, but now I'm breathing heavily. Roy sees me and jumps out of his chair, his face unsure and nervous. As I approach him, it's as though everything had just happened. We're back to Valentine's

Day, three years ago, when I woke up to nothing but a card and a broken heart. And now, here we are, different, and yet, the same.

"I'm sorry for calling you like this," he says, his gray eyes intently looking at me.

I sit down. He does the same.

I can see he's uncomfortable, and so am I. He's nervous, and I am, too. It's amazing how intimate and open we were to each other when we were together. Now here we are, like strangers again.

"Do you want some coffee?" he asks.

"No, I'm fine," I manage to say. I lean back and fold my arms. "So, let's talk," I say, avoiding his eyes.

"I can see you're still mad at me. I expected that," he says, glaring at the table.

"I was fine. At least I thought I was. But hearing your voice and seeing you now, I can't help but remember that *lovely* day," I reply, my eyes searching for a distraction.

He looks out the window and taps the sides of his coffee cup, searching for words to save our awkward exchange.

"It wasn't easy to leave you. I know it was unfair and you didn't deserve that."

"Why did you leave?" I blurt.

As I wait for him to reply, I realize that I didn't just walk into a café. I walked right into our past.

"I-I left you for many reasons." He clears his throat. "I was afraid you wanted marriage, and I wasn't ready for that. I liked you a lot, but I was confused about what I wanted. I had no idea how to tell you how I felt without committing to you."

There it was. He was afraid of commitment.

"Why couldn't you tell me that? I would've understood," I reply. But would I have really?

He looks away and rubs his shaved head.

"I was a coward, Al. I'll be the first to admit it, and I'm sorry." He glances up at me. "I'm sorry. I don't know what else to say or how to say it. I messed up," he says, shaking his head.

I could hear the sincerity in his voice. Is this the apology I've been waiting for all these years? Is this the closure Cindy has been talking about?

"I wish I could say it's OK, Roy, but it's not that easy. I accept your apology, but I'm not ready to forget about what happened," I say at last.

Maybe I said too much.

"I missed you a lot since I left that morning, but I couldn't go back to you because I was afraid you wouldn't even take me back or much less, speak to me."

I wanted to say more, but I let him talk. Again, he owed me this much.

"I always hoped you were OK, that you were coping fine. If it's any consolation, I broke my heart the day I left you. And I haven't been with anyone since."

My lips tighten when I realize we have both been unattached and thinking of each other all these years.

"Say something," he says, staring at the table with an uncomfortable smile.

"You broke my heart, Roy. A part of me still hates you for it," I say, swallowing hard.

He looks up at me, his eyes peering.

"That's fair. Trust me, I've been wanting to call you all this time, but I was afraid you had put me behind you. I took a chance when I called you today." He glances away and back at me. "Can I please buy you a cup of coffee or something?" he asks, a bit frazzled.

I exhale. "Sure. A latte would be great."

He gets up, and I watch him proceed to the counter. There is something so vulnerable about the way he looks and the way he talks. I'm not saying I've forgiven him, but there is a huge possibility I may eventually. Maybe I have to forgive him in order to move on. Despite how strange it was to hear from him today, I'm glad he called. I guess a late apology is better than no apology at all.

He sits back down and carefully rests a white giant mug on the table.

"You look great, by the way," he says.

"Thanks." I smile weakly. "You shaved your head," I say, wrapping my hands around the hot beverage.

"Yeah, I did. My hair's been like this for two years now," he says, nodding. He glances out the window. "You still live up there," he says, looking at my building, my bedroom window visible from where we're sitting.

"Yeah, I like my place, despite certain memories," I reply facetiously.

He shakes his head. "Ah, that hurts," he says. "But I deserve that."

"Anyway, what have you been up to?" I ask, changing the subject.

"I finished my third novel," he says proudly, his face relaxing a little.

"Congratulations," I say, with a quick smile.

"What about you? What's been keeping you busy these days?"

"Just my column," I reply dryly.

"You write a column?"

"I do. For *Trend Magazine.*"

44

"That's great, Al!" he says, smiling. "I knew you would get the job."

Roy knows how much I've been wanting to write for *Trend.* I must have told him a hundred times back when we were together. He was always very supportive of my goals, and I loved that about him.

"Thanks," I say, biting my tongue. A part of me wants to tell him that *Trend* called and offered me the job right after he left me, but before I could say anything, Roy says he's happy for me. Then he smiles and takes a sip of his coffee. I do the same and look away.

When I fix my eyes on Roy, my knees weaken.

7

Roy

As we sit here talking, I can't help but wonder if he called simply to apologize, or if there was a chance he wanted to get back together. Of course, that would never work. I can't let him back into my life. *No way.* But why can't I stop gazing at him every chance I get? I can't ignore how good he looks right now. His skin naturally tanned and his shaved head revealing his gorgeous face. He is wearing a white crew neck T-shirt that hides beneath his gray angora cardigan, which traces his fit frame. His straight cut jeans reveal his rugged side with a small rip on his left knee. His dark brown worn out leather shoes complete his attire. As much as I hated what he did to me, I can't help but still be attracted to him. But why?

I need to be strong. Danielle warned me about this. She knew seeing him could bring back old feelings. But are these old feelings? Or am I feeling this way because I miss being with someone and it has nothing to do with

Roy?

We both finish our coffee. Roy continues to tell me about his book and how long it took him to write it and edit it. I listen to him as the café becomes vacant.

"What about you? Aside from your column, are you writing anything else?" he asks.

"I dabble. I jot down notes here and there. I still want to write a book, but the inspiration hasn't found me."

"Maybe you need to get out there and find your inspiration. Maybe travel," he says.

"Travel," I repeat, as the thought about the matchmaker article lingers in my head.

"Why not? Sometimes, it's the only way to experience life and see what's out there."

I nod and contemplate telling him that I *do* have plans to travel—that Paris is on my itinerary, but there's no reason why he would need to know that.

"Yeah, it might be a good reason to get me out of here, and get out there."

"Definitely." He smiles. "Where would you go?"

"I don't know. Maybe somewhere in Italy or Spain?" I say, but Paris is the only place on my mind.

"Spain is beautiful. I was in Barcelona and Madrid last year. I was there for the summer. I saw some crazy bull fighting," he says.

What a coincidence. I spent the summer fighting the bulls in my heart too. The bulls won.

"Must've been fun," I say.

"It was interesting. I went with my dad. It was fun at the beginning, then we eventually got into each other's nerves," he says, managing a laugh.

I've never met Roy's dad, but he always talked about him. He was an English professor before he retired a few years ago. He is also a writer and has a few published books of his own.

"I can imagine. But someday you'll look back on it and realize that it was probably one of the best times of your life."

"Yeah, I know. I'm glad we made that trip. My dad's not getting any younger."

I smile.

He clears his throat.

"Are you dating anyone right now?" he says, changing the subject. Before I can even reply, he says, "I just want to be sure I'm not taking you away from someone by having you here with me."

What do I say? Should I lie? Maybe I should tell him I'm engaged. No, I should tell him I'm married—with two kids. No, three kids.

"I'm not with anyone right now," I say, unable to lie.

"That makes two of us," he says.

"Oh," I say, as our eyes meet.

We stay quiet for a few seconds.

"Why does it feel as if the past just happened a few hours ago and not years ago?"

"Maybe because this isn't over. We're not over," he says.

"Trust me, Roy. We are."

He leans back and looks away.

"Is it though?" he says under his breath.

"What do you mean?" I say, perplexed by his question.

He simply shrugs and doesn't say anything.

"Wait, if that's what you're thinking, it's not going to happen. We can't start over after what happened," I say.

"I know I messed up, Al, but I think everyone needs a second chance. Don't you?"

Is this why he wanted to see me, because he wanted to apologize so we could get back together?

"Is this why you called? To get me back?"

"No," he says, dropping his head. "Believe me, I called *only* to apologize." He lifts his head and our eyes meet again, and I can't look away. "But seeing you here now made me realize that I still have feelings for you," he finishes.

As much as I hate to admit it, I know what he means. I came here to hear his apology, and I didn't expect to still have feelings for him either. But it does not matter because Roy and I will never happen again.

"You think you still have feelings for me, but it's only because we're here right now. They're leftover feelings that will leave with you when we say goodbye tonight," I say, impressed with myself. My weaker side isn't taking the lead.

"You've always been the stronger one. I admire that about you." He pauses. "But, Al, I still care for you. I know it's hard to believe, but please believe me. I'm willing to try, if you are," he says, his eyes gazing at me, waiting for an answer.

"No, Roy," I say, shaking my head. "We can't do this. You broke my heart once before, and I don't think I can take it if you broke my heart again." But when I finish, something strange happens. My weaker side slowly takes over, and I begin to wonder if I should give him a second chance. What if he genuinely still cares? We *did* have a good time together. And he's funny, charming, and intelligent. But he's also the one who dumped me on Valentine's Day and fled without a warning and took three years to apologize.

"I don't blame you for hating me, Al. And I know that what I'm about to say is a shot in the dark." He swallows hard. "But would you have dinner with me tomorrow? Please have dinner with me."

In my head, I'm saying, no. Absolutely not, but when I finally speak, my weaker side spits out. "Sure."

Roy's eyes light up.

What have I done?

"Come on, it's getting late. I'll walk you to your apartment," he offers, sounding content with my reply.

"OK," I say.

Danielle is going to yell at me. I am going to yell at me.

We both get up and exit the café. The brisk air greets us. I wrap my cashmere scarf around my neck and zip up my wool coat. I glance at Roy. He looks ridiculously good.

Why am I still attracted to him?

We make it to the front door of my building and I get butterflies in my stomach.

"I'll pick you up here at seven tomorrow night?" he says.

"Sure," I say, avoiding his eyes.

He takes a few steps closer, and my knees shake.

"Can I hug you?" he asks.

My weaker side makes me nod.

Bad Lana. You're supposed to be strong.

Roy comes over and wraps his arms around me. It doesn't change how much I still hate him. But I hug him back. Tight.

We let go eventually, with my lead. I scurry to the door and turn the key. I look back at him as I push the door open.

"Goodnight," he says, with a somber look.

"Goodnight," I repeat.

I shut the door, sprint to my apartment, head straight to my bedroom, and dial Danielle's number. I get her voicemail.

"Danielle, it's Lana. Where are you? I may have made a huge mistake. Call me." I hang up the phone and peek out the window. I watch Roy leave as my heart beats a mile a minute.

I should've left for Paris.

8

The Truth

My phone is buzzing. It's been buzzing for a while. I roll to my side and reach for it.

"Hello," I say, struggling to open my eyes.

"Peonies or tulips? I can't decide." It's Cindy.

"Peonies," I answer, keeping my eyes shut. "I just woke up. What time is it?"

"Good choice. That's what I was thinking. It's nine. I'm on Lexington between 88th and 89th," she says, without pausing.

"What are you doing there?" I say, dragging my voice.

"I'm waiting for my wedding coordinator," she says.

"Oh."

"She's late. I hate waiting," she says, grinding her teeth.

Then my mind wanders, and I forget to reply.

"Are you OK? You don't sound like yourself," she says, her tone changing.

I prop my pillows behind me and fall back.

"You won't believe who called me yesterday," I say, still unable to grasp what happened just hours ago.

"Who? Oh my god, who?" she asks, all excited.

"Roy," I blurt.

"What! What the hell did he want? What did you say? Did you hang up on him? You should've," she says, in a loud tone.

"How many cups of coffee have you had?"

"Two. Three. Who cares? Tell me what happened."

"I didn't hang up on him, but Danielle had the same idea you had. She happened to be on the other line."

"I would've hung up, Lana!"

"Well, too late. I didn't. We spoke and he begged me to see him. He wanted to come over to talk, but I didn't want him to."

"The nerve of that guy. He doesn't even deserve to see you," she says, in an angry tone.

"You may not like what I'm about to say next," I say, cringing.

"What happened? What?" she asks impatiently.

"I agreed to see him at the café across the street."

"Oh, Lana," she says, her voice simmering down. "Why?"

"Maybe for closure. You said I needed closure," I say, defending myself.

"Well, did you get closure?"

"I'm not sure."

"Clearly, you didn't. You'll know if you got closure." She sighs. "What happened next?"

"He apologized, and we started talking, and it felt kind of good."

"Kind of good? Have you lost your mind? Lana, this is the same guy who left you on Valentine's Day. The same guy who caused you anxiety and stomachaches every February, for the last three years. Wake up!"

Yes, I know all that. I am aware of all that. Like I said, I didn't expect to still have feelings for him.

"I never should've seen him. I told him he could tell me everything on the phone, but he persisted, so, I agreed to meet him."

"How did it end?"

"Uh, well…" How do I tell her I'm seeing him again without her judging me?

"Here's the thing," I say, struggling to explain myself.

"Oh, no," she says. "Did you sleep with him?"

"No!" I retort. "Absolutely not."

"OK, so what's the problem?"

"I-I'm kind of seeing him tonight," I say, cringing once more.

"Kind of seeing him again tonight? How does one kind of see a guy? Lana, I thought you hated him."

"I do hate him. I think. I don't know. He asked me out to dinner, and I said, yes. It's too late. I already said yes," I say, not making any sense.

Darn it. I can't stop thinking about Roy's eyes and his fit frame and his shaved head and that tight hug.

"I can say what I want, but it doesn't matter. You are going to do what you want," she says, giving up.

"No, you can't say that. I need your strength. I'm weak right now," I say, covering my face with my hand.

"Yes, you are. You're absolutely weak right now." She sighs. "If you see him tonight, please don't wear your heart on your sleeve. You can't let him know you still have feelings for him. And if you really believe he deserves a second chance, you have to make him work for it. But if I were you, he's history. Let him go. Let it all go."

"I know."

"Hold on. Is that my coordinator?" she pauses, "What is she doing lugging my wedding dress around? I need to go. I'll call you later," she says agitated.

I hang up the phone and lie on my back with my eyes closed. Roy's face appears vividly in my head—the way he looked at me and the intensity in his eyes last night. It was as if he had so much more to say, but he had said it all.

I sit up quickly, hoping to shake off Roy's memory. I look around and notice my suitcase on the floor.

What about Paris and the matchmaker?

Have I let that all go?

My phone buzzes. I check the screen. It's Roy. I take a deep breath.

"Hello?", I answer, pretending I didn't know he was on the other line.

"Hey, Al. It's Roy."

Why is he calling this early? Is he cancelling our dinner plans already?

"Hi."

"I just wanted to say good morning." He pauses. "Good morning."

"Good morning," I reply softly.

"I also wanted to thank you for giving me a chance to see you last night. It meant a lot."

My heart softens again. I'm afraid my weak side has officially taken over.

"Glad we did," I say.

Glad we did? What am I doing?

"I made a reservation for tonight. I hope Italian food is OK with you."

"Sounds wonderful."

"I'll see you at seven."

"See you then," I confirm.

I hang up the phone and fall flat on my stomach, my cheeks burning, and I can't stop smiling.

What's happening to me?

9

Ice Cream, I Scream

It's 5:30 p.m. and I haven't figured out what to wear tonight. I've been looking at all the clothes I had prematurely packed yesterday.

My phone rings. It's Danielle.

"Hey, Danielle," I answer.

"Cindy called me. I know everything," she says.

Why are they talking about me? Who am I kidding? Of course, they're talking about me. They're concerned about their weak friend.

"What did she tell you?" I ask.

"She told me about the dinner tonight. Are you sure about all this?"

"I don't know. We're going as friends," I explain.

"As friends? This guy broke your heart, Lana. You call that a friend?" she retorts.

"I know, I know. You don't have to remind me," I take a deep breath. "It's probably a mistake, but I already said yes."

"You know you could still cancel, right? People cancel all the time," she says.

"I could, but maybe I don't want to."

"I guess you don't."

"I guess so."

She sighs heavily.

"Please don't do anything silly," she warns.

"Like what?"

"Like fall back in love with him."

I sigh. I'm too confused right now.

"That's not going to happen," I say, but I'm not convinced by my own words.

"I'm off to prenatal yoga. Call me later."

"I will."

A pint of ice cream is necessary right about now, so, I take a quick trip to the corner store. This is all I need to clear my head—something cold and sweet.

As I'm leaving the store, I notice a familiar face go past me. I look back and realize it's Roy's friend, Dino. I haven't seen him since Roy and I broke up. We used to all hang out a lot. Dino is a pretty loud guy who loves to talk with his hands like a real Italian. He's the opposite of Roy. He's tall and stocky.

"Dino!" I yell out. He looks at me and his dark eyes widen.

"Lana? Holy shit! How've you been?" he says loudly. Exactly how I remembered him.

We approach each other, and he greets me with a warm hug.

"I'm good. How are you?"

"Great. What are you doing out here?" he asks.

"I live in this area," I explain.

"Oh, right. Well, I know it's been years, but I'm sorry about you and Roy." He shakes his head.

Does he know about Roy and I now?

"Yeah," I say, tightening my lips.

"I haven't talked to him in over a year. I moved to Queens. I'm only here because I dropped off my girl-friend at her friend's place a block away from here."

"Great."

"Man, I can't believe it's been years. What about you? Are you dating anyone? What's new with you?" he asks, smiling.

I'm not sure how to answer any of his questions. He obviously doesn't know about Roy and I. Should I tell him?

"I'm not dating anyone at the moment." I pause. "But I am meeting Roy for dinner tonight."

Dino's facial expression goes blank. He steps back and gives me an odd glare.

"What's wrong?" I ask.

He tilts his head.

"Nothing. I can't believe you guys are still talking."

"Oh, no. We're not really talking. He just called last night, and we met up for coffee. That was the first time we've spoken and seen each other since we broke up."

"But the way he just left you, Lana, that was pretty fucked up," he blurts.

I didn't expect Roy's friend to not be on his side. I thought guys always stuck by each other even when they didn't agree. I thought there was a secret code. This was unexpected. I guess he knew about Valentine's Day.

"Yeah, it was, but he explained everything to me last night, and he apologized."

"And you forgave him? Wow, you're something else, Lana," he says, still surprised.

"Let's just say I listened to his apology. But it may take some time for me to accept it."

"Well, hey, good for you guys. He's a lucky guy," he says, nodding his head.

"We're meeting for dinner tonight, but only as friends. We're not getting back together," I explain.

He surrenders his hands. "Hey, do whatever. It's your life, but remember this. You're a special girl…" he says, lowering his voice, his eyes gazing at me with concern.

I'm not used to hearing him talk like this.

Then he continues, "but between you and I, I didn't know about him cheating on you until long after you guys broke up. If I had known that, I would've told you myself."

My heart stops.

What did he say?

Roy cheated on me?

My face heats up. I nod at Dino, pretending I know about everything. But I don't know anything at all.

I squeeze the ice cream in my hand, imagining it's Roy's skull.

"Right. The cheating," I repeat, while screaming inside.

"He told me he couldn't live with the guilt and that's why he left you. But I'm sure he told you all of that."

I feign a smile, my lips burning with anger.

No, he didn't. He failed to mention all of that to me last night.

"Y-e-a-h," I say, forcing the word out.

I grind my teeth as steam comes out of my ears.

"Listen, I need to go. My ice cream is melting," I say, lifting up my little brown paper bag. Inside is Roy's crushed skull.

"Well, it was great seeing you. Tell that bastard I said what's up," he says.

Bastard.

"I will."

No. I won't.

I turn around and bolt back to my apartment.

10

Closure

The minute I get home, I shove the ice cream in the freezer, grab a throw pillow from the couch and cover my face and scream as loud as I can until I can't breathe. After a few good screams, I run to the bathroom and splash cold water on my face. I am beyond hurt. I am furious.

My phone won't stop ringing. It's Cindy and Danielle taking turns. A part of me wants to pick up the phone and tell them everything, but another part of me wants to be left alone.

Roy cheated on me. The coward cheated on me. The scared man lied. He couldn't face the truth. And that's why he left me. Then he decides to come back —three years later, with an apology that doesn't even apologize for anything. Why didn't he tell me all this last night? Is this why he asked me out to dinner tonight, so he could finally tell me what he's been hiding from me all these years?

I start running in place to calm myself down. The moment I start panting, I stop. All of a sudden, my mood changes. The rage inside of me fades, and I feel sorry for Roy. And a part of me wants to give him a second chance. But why? Where is this all coming from? Despite what I had heard today, why do I still want to see him? Is it because I am willing to forgive him? Or has my mere attraction to him blinded me? Because now I could care less about the rest. But how? Roy cheated on me. How could I have compassion for someone who has hurt me? Am I that desperate for something, or anything, that resembles a relationship or love?

Despite my confused state, I survey my bedroom for an outfit. Roy will be here in half an hour. After trying on a bunch of clothes, I settle on a long sleeve navy blue wrap-around dress. I even curl my hair. If Danielle and Cindy knew what I know now and how I still plan on going to dinner with Roy, they would assume I've lost my mind.

I'm standing in the middle of my room, staring at my clutter, wondering what has happened to me the last few days. I used to be organized. Now I have empty hangers all over the floor and a mountain of clothes on my bed. But despite the disaster that surrounds me, I don't bother to clean up. Instead, I watch the clock on my side table. *Tick tock, tick tock.* As the seconds pass, a wild sense of anxiety spreads throughout my body. I try to shake it off, but notice the pile of clothes again, and this time, it irritates me. I open my suitcase and begin shoving the clothes inside until my bed is clear. Then I drop the cover and push it to the corner. Somehow, this relieves me. I glance at the clock.

It's 7:00 p.m. I sit on the bed and check the curls in my hair with my fingers.

I should've listened to Danielle. She said I needed to be strong, and I wasn't. I can't believe I said yes to dinner.

It's 7:10 p.m. I peek out my bedroom window and catch a glimpse of Roy standing outside. I can feel the tension between us, even from four stories high.

My phone rings. It's him. I ignore it. He leaves a message.

I pace between the living room and my bedroom, still contemplating about dinner.

My phone beeps. It's a text from Roy saying he's downstairs.

I don't reply.

A few minutes later, my phone rings. It's Fred, our doorman, but I don't pick up. I don't know what to say. I keep seeing Dino's surprised reaction when I told him about tonight. I can't go to dinner with Roy. I already know what he's going to say. I know the truth. There's no point in seeing him now.

I switch my phone to silent. I pace again, my eyes darting from left to right.

I need to get out of here, or else, I am going to lose it.

I snatch my purse from the bed and toss my phone inside. I open the top drawer of my dresser. I take my phone charger and my passport and shove them all in my purse, along with my keys and a scarf.

It's time I do what I should've done days ago.

I zip up my suitcase and roll it to the door. My phone buzzes. I check it. It's my editor. I shove my phone back in my bag. Sorry, I've already checked out. I open the door and hoist my suitcase out and let the door slam behind me. I speed through the hallway and drag my suitcase four flights down. I exit out the back way. A cab happens to stop in front of me dropping off passengers. I snag it and demand to be dropped off at the airport.

We drive past the front of my building where I see Roy waiting for me. He can wait all night.

How's that for closure?

11

Changing Lanes

The cab ride to the airport is not going as smoothly as I want it to. We're stuck in traffic, and I can't see past the delivery truck in front of us. My legs are itching to get out and run.

"I hope this traffic clears up soon," I say to the stocky cab driver, enjoying his gyro. The tzatziki sauce drips down his dark beard and he wipes it off with his hairy forearm. His sweat has formed an odd shape on the back of his white short-sleeved button-down shirt. He isn't bothered at all by the traffic, and why should he be anyway? He's not the one trying to escape.

"Soon," he says, while chewing.

He takes a quick sip of his canned soda and gulps loudly.

"Thanks," I reply.

It's been at least ten minutes since we last moved. Fortunately, it's not like I'm about to miss a flight, because I didn't book anything. Unfortunately, sitting here in this uncomfortable seat and listening to the cab driver, munch, swallow, and gulp, while I wait for us to move, is not the most fun either. But it's better than being with Roy.

The cab driver turns on his radio. Heavy metal music that I've never heard before is playing at medium volume. I glance out the window and notice an empty cab next to us in traffic. I wish I could get out and move to that one instead, but I can't. My suitcase is in the trunk.

As I imagine myself pulling off a silly stunt, the cab moves, and the radio shuts off.

"We're moving," the cab driver announces.

"Great," I reply.

We're making progress. The cab driver is no longer eating or drinking and his radio has stayed off. The traffic has cleared and we're moving smoothly. I lean back on my seat.

My phone hasn't buzzed in a while. But I'm sure it won't be long until it does. I hope it will be Cindy or Danielle, because I can't wait to tell them about my closure with Roy. Seeing Dino made me realize that I deserve more. I don't need Roy. I don't want Roy. It doesn't matter how good-looking he is, or how firm his arms are and how great he smells. It doesn't matter how clean he looks and how gorgeous his eyes are and how beautiful his smile is. And who cares about that warm and comforting hug from him last night anyway? *AAAAAAHHHHH!* Why am I still attracted to him?

As my thoughts drive me crazy, the driver slams on the brakes and jolts us back.

What's going on?

"Why did we stop?" I ask.

He looks at me through the rear-view mirror and points out the window at the traffic. Then he rips opens a bag of potato chips and turns the radio back on.

NO!

12

Airport

After listening to the driver's heavy metal music playing in full blast for over an hour, we make it to the airport.

It hasn't been easy since I arrived. I've been here now for a couple of hours doing my best to flee the country. Here's a tip. If you're trying to book a last-minute flight, while you're in a rush, enraged, brokenhearted, agitated, irritated, and hungry, you're better off not doing so. I've done things I don't usually do. I raised my voice at the lady behind the counter when she told me I had just missed the last flight to Paris when it wasn't her fault. I cursed out a guy for cutting in line when I was waiting to buy coffee. Then I pushed a group of people out of my way, while I ran to book the last flight to Amsterdam. I barely made it. I'm not proud of myself. But I'm desperate for a ticket out of here. There is no way I am going back home. Flying to Amsterdam and taking a three-hour train ride to Paris is better than sitting here, waiting until tomorrow for the next flight. Skipping off to another place as soon as possible is the only way I can forget about everything. And I can't wait to leave.

My voicemail reminder beeps. It could be Craig or Cindy or Danielle. Or it could be Roy. I don't bother checking.

I take a seat next to my gate. As I stare at the geometric patterned carpet, I remember Roy's apology from last night. It lingers in my head like a bad commercial jingle repeating itself over and over. I can't shut it up.

Shut up!

My phone buzzes incessantly. The guy next to me clears his throat. He's annoyed. I'm annoyed. We're all annoyed. But I still don't check my phone.

The gate agent announces that we're boarding in fifteen minutes. Finally, some good news.

If I had left for Paris the day I had planned to, I could've avoided all of this. But maybe all this was meant to happen. If I didn't go out to get ice cream, I would've never seen Dino, and I would've not found out about the truth. But then again, if I went to dinner with Roy, maybe he would've told me everything. I guess I'll never know. It's sickening to think that I spent close to three years wallowing over my breakup with Roy, suffering yearly stomachaches, and despising a holiday I used to love—all because of him. Then I finally find a reason to move on—Paris, but end up hearing from Roy, seeing Roy, almost forgiving Roy, and unexpectedly, almost falling back in love with Roy.

I should've left for Paris when I said I would.

It's five minutes to boarding time, and the voicemail reminder on my phone persists like Roy's sorry apology in my head. I dig my hand inside my purse and yank out my phone. I punch in my password. The first message is from Roy.

"Hey, it's Roy. I hope you didn't forget about tonight. I'm downstairs."

Second message.

"It's me again. I'm getting worried. Are you OK? Are *we* OK?"

Third message.

"I'm at the café across the street." He pauses. "Listen, I get it. You didn't forget about tonight. You changed your mind. I guess I deserve this. I knew it was too good to be true that you said yes to dinner. I get it." He sighs. "I-I wanted to tell you something that should've been said a long time ago. I-I just didn't know how to." He clears his throat. "I guess this is my chance now. Not the way I wanted to go about this, but here it goes." He clears his throat again.

And in a shaky voice, pausing several times in between, he reveals the real reason why he broke up with me. He says he made a huge mistake. And he couldn't face me after that.

"I'm sorry, Al. You have no idea how many times I've sat awake at night regretting what I did, wishing I could take it all back and do everything differently. But I can't. I have so much guilt inside of me, whether you believe me or not, it's the truth. I only wanted you. Now I can't even have you," he says, his voice cracking, stressing every word. "But I guess it's too late for all this now. I'm sorry."

I hit delete, slip the phone back in my purse, and board the plane.

You're right, Roy. It's too late.

13

Springs

As the plane takes off, I look out the window and watch the view beneath us become smaller and smaller. My eyes settle on the bright lights illuminating the city below. My heavy heart lightens as if a weight has been lifted off my chest, and I can now breathe. As the dark clouds cover the city and darkness is all I see, I pull the shades down and lean back on my seat. Roy's voicemail becomes a distant memory. When it's too late, there's no need for contemplation or explanation. It no longer deserves any of that. It's been over for Roy and I. It's been over for three years. His confession today was for him—not for me. It was for him to release the guilt he's been feeling all these years. He needed to do it to appease himself. I realize that now. Roy didn't want me back. That was his guilt taking over, making him believe that despite all these years, he still wanted to be with me. I guess I wasn't the only one who needed closure. He needed it, too. Now we can both move on.

A few hours later, I wake up and notice the young lady sitting next to me. She appears uneasy, flipping her blonde hair to the right and to the left and then leans back on her chair and bounces off as if she has springs attached to her back. She glances at me every few minutes and leans back and bounces off again. How long can she keep this up for?

The next time she turns to me, I smile.

She smiles back.

"How's it going?" I say, with no intention of having a conversation, but talking to her might be the only way to stop her from fidgeting.

Her face lights up, and she settles in her seat.

"It's good... I think," she says, crossing her legs. "Is Amsterdam your final stop?" she asks.

"Yes," I say, but it's not.

"Me, too. I'm going to a bachelor party."

I furrow my eyebrows. "A bachelor party?"

She chuckles.

"I know what you're thinking. Yes, it's for guys. My boyfriend's there right now for a bachelor party. He doesn't know I'm going," she says, with her eyes suspiciously darting from left to right.

"Oh." I guess that kind of says it all, doesn't it?

She's silent for a few seconds and then blurts, "It's not what you think. I'm not going there to spy on him." She laughs. "And I'm not a stripper."

"OK," I reply with what I hope is an assuring smile.

"I'm going because I want to tell him that I'm leaving him," she continues.

I feel my eyebrows raise.

"I'm sorry, did I confuse you?" she asks.

"A bit," I say with a shrug. "I hope you don't mind me asking, but why go all the way to Amsterdam to tell him you're leaving him? Couldn't you wait until he got back?" I know I shouldn't care, but now I'm curious.

"I can't tell him when he gets back." She pauses. "Because I won't be there. I'm not coming back. After I see him in Amsterdam, I'm moving to Italy."

"You're moving to Italy?" I repeat, finding myself sucked into her story.

She fiddles with her fingers.

"Yes, I am. I'm in love," she says.

Great. This is exactly what I need right now. Another cheater. Ladies and gentlemen, we have a cheater on the plane. Hold on to your hearts.

"You're in love with another man?" I ask.

"No," she laughs. "I'm in love with Italy," she says, her face glowing.

She goes on to tell me that she's always loved Italy, and that her father is originally from Rome. They used to visit every summer when she a little kid. She said she's always wanted to move there, but her boyfriend never liked the idea. As a matter of fact, he never likes any of her ideas. Meanwhile, she agrees with everything he says while he dismisses everything she says.

"I need to be free for a while," she says. "We are not right for each other. We never were. So, when he told me, not asked me, he was going to his friend's bachelor party in Amsterdam, I figured it was the best time for me to leave him. I've been hanging on for the last six months looking for a way out—this is my chance. I've grown to hate him more than I have grown to love him. I need to end our relationship before I hate him too much that I begin to hate myself." She turns to me. "Do you think it's foolish for me to do it this way?"

Why does my opinion even matter? I'm a stranger on a plane. But I see her eyes desperate for a reply, so, I take a shot.

"I think it's a daring move. But if that's what your heart desires, then you should go for it."

"You mean showing up in Amsterdam to break up with him or moving to Italy?" she asks, intently looking at me.

"Uh… well, everything," I reply, not sure I gave her the answer she wanted to hear, or the answer she needed to hear.

"I hope it's not stupid of me to surprise him in Amsterdam. Maybe I should've left him a note instead like I had originally planned," she says, doubting her next move.

Left him a note? Sounds too familiar. Flashbacks of Roy and Valentine's Day comes crashing down on me, and I get all worked up.

"Listen, we don't know each other, but you asked me for my opinion, so I'm going to give it to you." I scoot down to the edge of my seat and turn to face her. "Your story reminds me of mine. Unfortunately, I was the one who received the note. It wasn't easy being on the receiving end of it. Whether you do it in Amsterdam or not— no matter how you end it, it's going to hurt either way."

The words left me, and there was no stopping them. She's planning to leave her boyfriend to fulfill a dream and end a relationship that was clearly not working out. What is so wrong with that? And why do I care? I don't know her, or the man she's leaving. Why does it bother me and affect me at all?

I watch her lean back on her chair in slow motion. This time, with no springs attached.

14

Space Cakes and Spacing Out

After a smooth flight, but a bumpy emotional ride, we land in Amsterdam Airport Schiphol. I collect my belongings and exit the plane. The lady who sat next to me never said a word again throughout the trip. I wonder if she is still going through with her plans. After all, she came all the way here.

I pass customs. Next stop is the train station. On my way there, I realize I left my laptop at home. The thought leaves me restless. Everything I need is in there. How am I supposed to write, now? On second thought, maybe I won't need to. At least not after that last article I emailed to Craig.

When I reach the Amsterdam Central Station, I check the monitor and search for the next train to Paris. I purchase my ticket and proceed to the platform, checking the time on my phone every couple of minutes. My hands clamp up, and my emotions run wild. I am anxious about the unknown, the mysterious café that I will soon discover. I imagine it will be hidden in a small alley where only a few people can find it, a place where a line of single hopefuls will extend out the door. Rain or shine, they will brave the cold or sweat the heat, patiently waiting for their turn—expecting to heal their broken hearts and crush all painful memories of past loves. Where the inevitable will be an introduction to a new love that will last for as long as the world exists. And when my turn comes, I will stroll inside in a beautiful dress and a red coat, and all the single men will turn to look at me, except for one. And he will be the one.

The train station isn't as crowded as I had expected. But then again, I don't know what I expected. For starters, I didn't expect to be in Amsterdam. This is what happens with lack of planning and a little bit of insanity. Looking back at how I stormed out of my apartment, avoiding Roy and the doorman, escaping from the back exit, just shows how desperate I was to flee. Now here I am, next to a group of guys in hooded sweatshirts talking about space cakes and coffee shops.

I shuffle through my purse, making sure my passport is in a spot that's easy to get to. I have always been an organized person. I never leave the house unless I know everything is in its place. My books always lined up, my cereal boxes in alphabetical order. Even my purse resembles a filing cabinet, complete with compartments. And now everything is somewhere else. But somehow, I'm fine with it.

The train arrives. I hop on behind a crowd of eager tourists. I choose the window seat on a vacant row closest to the exit. When I get settled, the train hisses and slowly pulls out of the station.

I'm finally on my way to Paris.

I retrieve the matchmaker article from my purse and read it until I memorize every word. Then I think about Sylvia and her relationship. What if it didn't last? And what about all the other folks who were matched? Where are they now, and are they still in love with the same person? Or have they strayed and found other lovers? I glance back at the article, and this time, my eyes land on the date on top of the page.

March 25, 1995.

This was written over a decade ago. My shoulders slump forward. What if the café no longer exists? What am I doing going all the way to Paris for?

There's an older man looking at me. Let me rephrase that. He's staring at me. I stow the article back in my purse and glance out the window. I can see the man's reflection, but now he's looking down focused on something like he's writing or reading a book. I stare out at the view, and it's like looking at a thousand photographs zipping past us. As I admire each photograph flipping quickly, I notice the same man looking at me again. Minutes later, my eyes fold. And somewhere between Amsterdam and Brussels, I fall asleep.

A cold breeze blows past my row and wakes me. I open my eyes. There's a piece of paper on the empty seat next to me. I reach for it. It's a drawing of a woman in deep thought, gazing out a window. I look closer. My eyes widen. It's a drawing of me. I lean forward and scan the passengers, wondering who drew me. As I search for the artist, I notice that the older man who was staring at me before is gone. I guess that's why he kept looking. But why did he pick me?

I lean back, studying the details of the drawing. The eyes are searching, the forehead wrinkled, and the lips pouting. It's me. And I look confused, anxious, and sad.

He has captured my every emotion. As I continue to stare at the image, I notice his signature on the bottom right corner.

Philippe Renard.

Below it, it says, *Enjoy Love. Enjoy Paris.*

I press the drawing against my chest. "Enjoy Love. Enjoy Paris," I repeat quietly to myself.

I fold the portrait and tuck it inside my purse. I push my head back and shut my tired eyes.

15

Halt!

I wake up from a screeching halt.

The train has stopped. I can hear murmurs from the passengers. I open my eyes and realize the seats are all filled. Some people are standing and peeking out the window, while others are wrestling with their belongings.

"We're a few feet away from the station," announces the young lady sitting next to me. I could tell from her accent that she's American. Her hair is short and dyed unevenly red, her oversized sunglasses covering most of her face. She's wearing a black coat and fitted jeans that cover her skinny frame.

"Thanks," I say, straightening up in my seat. "Do you know what happened?"

"Something mechanical, as usual. They said it should only take a few minutes."

"Too bad we couldn't make it a few feet before it broke down," I say, with a brief laugh, trying to lighten the mood.

She manages to chuckle with no emotion. "You're American," she says.

"Yes." I smile. "I'm from New York. Where are you from?"

"Chicago. But I live in Paris," she says, dragging her voice.

"How do you like Paris?" I ask, perking up in my seat.

Her jaw tightens. "I hate it. I need to get out of there," she says, glaring out the window.

I didn't expect to hear such a harsh response.

"Oh, that's too bad," I say, not knowing how else to react.

Then she turns to me with her dark sunglasses.

"I moved to Paris because of my Parisian boyfriend," she says sarcastically. "But we broke up last week." She looks away. "I can't stand him. I hate everything about him. I hate Paris," she says, in a low and deep voice.

"I'm sorry to hear that," I say.

"Don't be sorry. It's hard to understand. Our relationship was complicated. He's married," she explains, without pausing.

"He's married?" I repeat.

"Yes. He told me he would leave her, but he went back to her a few months later. I should've known," she says, shaking her head.

I tighten my lips. I don't know how else to respond. What do you say to a stranger who is obviously hurting?

She looks at me, and I can see the tears rolling past her glasses. She mops them off quickly with her hands.

"I know what you're thinking. I am an absolute fool for dating a married man."

"Oh, no, I didn't say or think that at all. I am not judging you," I respond defensively.

82

"See, the thing is, when I met him I didn't know he was married. He and I went out for weeks and he never said a word about his wife, and I never saw a ring. How was I supposed to know? By the time he revealed everything to me, I was already too in love with him to leave. Maybe I'm just a stupid girl." She shakes her head. "Because when he promised me he was leaving her, I believed him. Can you believe it? I believed him!" she says, her voice getting deeper and louder.

I want to empathize with her. I do. But she's slowly sucking out all the excitement I have for my trip.

"It's not your fault. At least now you know," I say, trying to comfort her, at the same time, hoping my turning away would discourage her from talking to me.

But she continues.

"I mean, why was I so blind and so stupid?" she says, with rage in her voice.

I turn back to face her. "You may have been blind because you loved him, but that doesn't make you stupid," I say, realizing I am now her therapist.

"I gave up everything to move to Paris. I wanted a fairy tale, and I got a fucking heartache."

Hold on. Aren't I going to Paris for a fairy tale, too? Am I chasing something that doesn't exist? Should I turn back now and save myself?

"How did you meet, if you don't mind me asking?" I'm not sure why I asked. I'm supposed to cut this conversation short, but now I've managed to prolong it. I can't help it. Now I'm curious. What if they met at the café with the matchmaker? I need to know.

"I came to Paris with a few friends for a week-long vacation. I met him at a party, and we hooked up that night."

"Were you instantly attracted to each other?"

Seriously, why am I still asking her questions?

"Yes, we were. I spent the next few days with him. Then I had to leave to go back to Chicago. We exchanged emails and through emails alone, he managed to talk me into moving to Paris." She puts her hand on her forehead and shakes her head.

"Do you think everything happened too quickly?"

I'm doing it again.

"Of course, it did. I moved out of Chicago and left everything I had because I was a fucking idiot. I left everything. Everything! Now I'm buried in debt with no job, and I need to move back home." She grabs her purse and pulls out a cigarette, eager to smoke it.

Before I can say anything, she looks at me and says, "Have you ever had your heart broken like this? It's horrible." This time, her voice is even louder.

Will this train ever move?

"I've had my heart broken many times," I reply, hoping this would, in some way, ease her pain because I know telling her about my pathetic Valentine's Day sob story won't. Besides, I'm not one to share my personal stories with strangers.

"Don't be fooled by the accent. Don't be fooled by their good looks. Don't let them melt you with their words and trick you. Don't sleep with them on the first night. Don't do it. Don't ever do it. Parisian men are horrible. They're horrible." Each word she says with repulsion.

How could she feel this way about Parisian men and generalize all of them? As far as I know, she's only dated one. But what do I know about her anyway? This is my first time going to Paris. With my luck, I can't even get there. The train still has not moved.

"I'll remember that," I say, wondering if the Parisian women on the train agree or if the Parisian men disagree and want to curse us American women out.

This heavy conversation must end now.

"I hope we move soon," I say, changing the subject.

She crosses her arms and in a stern voice says, "I hope this train never moves."

Please, train. MOVE!

16

Room 210

We arrive at the Paris Nord Train Station at 2:38 p.m. Before I could bid farewell to my fellow broken-hearted American, she had already left her aisle seat and maneuvered quickly out the door without ever looking back at me. She didn't even have a suitcase. Where is she going now? Where will she stay? More importantly, where am I going, and where am I going to stay?

I exit the train and make my way through the bustling crowd, witnessing several arrivals and departures. As loud announcements, babies crying, and people chattering fill the air, I grow eager and excited about my trip. Despite the way I left New York and the negative remarks of the lady I met on the train about Paris and Parisian men, I still want to believe in romance and in love. She was furious, as furious and hurt as I was when Roy left me, and I understand that. I hope her broken heart eventually heals.

Will mine ever?

On my way out the station, a tall lady with big hair walks past me and rushes out the door. She lights up a cigarette and exhales with a loud sigh of relief, as if she had been deprived of nicotine for months.

The moment I exit the train station, the cold air rejuvenates me. I wrap my scarf around my neck and button up my coat. I drag my suitcase toward a long taxi line, as the crowd behind me grows. Are they all here to see the Eiffel Tower, or are they here to look for love?

My eyes sting from the glare outside. I reach inside my purse for my sunglasses. As I do, the middle-aged couple in front of me, holding matching Louis Vuitton suitcases, smile and start talking to me. They ask me how long I'm staying in Paris. I give them a squinted and frazzled look.

"A few days. Short trip," I say, continuing to dig my hand inside my purse.

"Where are you staying?" the wife asks.

"We own a small apartment on Saint-Germain-des-Prés. We bought it after our first trip here several years ago. We knew we would always come back," the husband says, putting his arm around his wife. She proudly kisses his cheek.

I nod, still searching for my sunglasses. This time, I check my pockets.

"Are you OK, hon?" the wife asks, her hand now on my arm.

I smile. "I'm fine. I just can't find my sunglasses."

"They're on your head," she points out.

"Oh," I laugh, and quickly reach for them and put them on. "Thank you," I say, my cheeks flushed.

"Is this your first time in Paris?" she asks.

"Yes, it is," I say, nodding.

"Oh, you'll love it here. It's very romantic," she says, stressing the word *very*. "And the food is fantastic. Really fantastic," she says, smiling. Her husband agrees as she wraps her arms around his large waist.

"I have a feeling I'll like it here, too," I say with a smile, relieved to have met the happy couple. I pull my suitcase forward as the line speeds toward the front.

Minutes later, the happy couple waves at me as they hurry to their cab. The husband tells his wife to get in, but she helps him roll their bags instead. The cab driver comes out and offers to take their bags so he could put them in the trunk, but the husband demands he does it himself. The wife then tells her husband to let the cab driver load the car, but the husband still refuses. Soon, the perfect couple is arguing. They continue to argue, while I hop on the next cab. I tell the driver to take me to the Shakespeare and Company bookstore. He nods and loads my suitcase in the back. When he shuts the trunk, I see the couple through the rear-view mirror. I watch as they board their cab, but only after the husband had loaded the trunk himself.

As we drive away, I feel as though I have lost all access to my emotions. Like my feelings have taken a break. Maybe I'm in shock, because I can't believe I've left everything behind to come here.

I crack the window open and stare out like a little kid, enjoying the wind against my face. Minutes later, we drive past the Louvre and down boulevards with cafés and shops and restaurants. My heart races, and I can't stop smiling. My eyes dart from one corner to another, as I try to savor every scene that zips past us.

"Your first time in Paris?" the cab driver asks, half of his face covered with a thick dark beard.

"Yes, it is," I reply.

"Where are you from?" he asks.

"New York."

"Ah, New York, The Big Apple, The City that Never Sleeps," he says, his eyes lighting up.

"That's the one," I say, smiling.

"I lived there once," he says, proudly.

"How did you like New York?"

"It was great. I was young. I met many women."

"Great," I say.

"But it was only for the summer. I came back to Paris and married my neighbor," he explains.

"That's wonderful. How long have you been married?"

"Not long. That was twenty years ago," he says, with a laugh. "She left me for another man."

That's awful. Why is he laughing? It's not funny.

"I'm sorry to hear that," I say.

"No problem," he laughs once more. "I am living the way I was living in New York. Many girlfriends, lots of sex, and no commitments," he says, laughing out loud.

Way too much information for me, guy.

"Great," I say, not knowing how else to reply. I'm not about to ask him about love, etcetera. The man is obviously happy where he is, and good for him.

"New York, New York," he sings out loud. Then he pauses. *"Madame,* the Seine River," he points out, glancing at me in the rear-view mirror.

I gaze out at the water, and quickly fall into a daydream.

A few minutes later, we pull up to a curb.

"Voilà," he says. "Shakespeare and Company, *Madame."* He swings his door open, pops the trunk, and leaves

my suitcase on the sidewalk. I exit the cab, pay him, and thank him.

"Merci, Madame," he says, and jumps back in the cab and drives away.

If I felt numb earlier, I don't anymore. Because here I am next to a black lamppost on Rue de la Bucherie with my heart pounding in my chest. Across the street from where I'm standing, the grand façade of the Notre Dame Cathedral is staring back at me. I take a long deep breath as my eyes settle on the white fluffy clouds above. I turn my head to the right, and I see the Shakespeare and Company bookstore.

My landmark.

My beginning.

I want to run in and scan the books, smell the pages, read the words, but I am quickly reminded of why I am here. So, I turn around and focus on finding a place to stay. I scurry away from the bookstore and within minutes, stumble upon a hotel with a narrow entrance. It has a yellow awning and two giant potted plants by the glass doors. I enter the quaint little hotel tucked between two souvenir shops.

"Bonjour, Madame," greets a tall lady at the front desk. Her dark hair is pulled up in a tight bun. She is wearing a beige suit with a small floral pin on the left side of her jacket and a nametag that reads, "Josephine."

"Bonjour," I say, hating the way I pronounced the word. "I'm looking for a room, please."

"One person?" she asks.

"Yes," I reply, moving my suitcase closer to me.

She nods her head and looks at the screen in front of her.

"*Voilà.* We have a room for you on the second floor. It will be 180 Euros a night," she says.

"I'll take it."

"How long will you be staying?" she asks.

Good question. I don't know.

"Umm, until next Sunday," I say, but I'm not sure.

I pull out my wallet and hand her my credit card. She slides it through the machine and gives it back to me with a smile.

"*Merci.* You are all set. Your room is on the second floor. Room 210."

"Room 210," I repeat. "Thank you. Do you have a map of the city?" I ask.

"*Oui.*" She grabs a map and unfolds it. "We are here," she says, circling our hotel with her pen. "Let us know if you have any questions." She hands me the map and an actual key, not a keycard.

"Thank you so much," I say, tucking the map and the key inside my coat pocket.

I turn around and pull my suitcase toward the elevator. Except, there is no elevator. Or at least I can't find it. But what I do spot is a long staircase draped with old floral carpet, that once upon a time, had a darker shade of red.

I return to the front desk where Josephine has just hung up the phone.

"Excuse me?" I say.

She sees me and smiles. "*Oui, Madame?*"

"Where is the elevator?"

"I am sorry, *Madame*, we don't have an elevator. We apologize. You have to take the stairs," she says, and points toward the dreary staircase.

"Oh, I see. Thank you," I say, rolling my suitcase back.

If I had planned this trip ahead of time, I would have probably booked a hotel with an elevator. Unfortunately, none of this was planned, and I don't have time to look around for a different hotel. This will have to do.

After lugging my suitcase up a flight of stairs, I pass five doors before locating my room. Room 210. I turn the key and push the door open with my elbows and proceed inside. The room is tiny and everything inside is red. The bed is dressed with a red quilt with a white sheet peeking out. The headboard is in red velvet, and leaning against it, are two red square pillows sitting far apart from each other. Floral wallpaper covers the walls and a black, rotary phone sits on a tiny antique side table.

I drop my bags on the floor.

I'm here.

17

Le Café Dubois

I freshen up then head down to the lobby, holding the magazine article with one hand and the map with the other. I speed past the empty front desk and exit the glass doors. The cold breeze greets me with a big embrace. I make a right and begin my journey.

My palms are sweating. The farther I go, I become more anxious and nervous. Despite the anxiety bursting inside of me, I cannot wait to join the line of single hopefuls standing outside the café waiting for their turn to find love. If it happened to Sylvia, then maybe there is a chance it could also happen to me.

When I arrive in front of the Shakespeare and Company bookstore, I unfold the article and go over the directions one more time. I try to focus, but find myself happily distracted by the sights around me. I pass beautiful old apartment buildings, quaint restaurants and bistros, and a row of gift shops with colorful scarves on display out on the sidewalk, as tourists and locals walk to and fro.

I check my directions again, and this time, manage to stay on track. I make a right into an alley, and when I do, my feet dance on the cobblestones, my heart light as a feather. I stroll along as though I've been here before.

Soon, all I hear are my own footsteps. Quiet streets could only mean one thing. I'm getting closer.

As I proceed down the peaceful alley, a car comes out of nowhere and lays their horn at me. I leap onto the sidewalk, and by the time I turn around, the car is gone. I shake it off and continue along the little path. I speed up and almost miss the narrow alley. I pause to consult the directions on the article one more time.

I'm getting closer.

I follow the alley as it curves left. I search for a doorway, but so far, all I see are colorful walls and windows. And then I notice a beautiful old red frame door, sitting by itself in the middle of the alley.

This is it.

I breathe heavily. And in one slow motion, I lift my head with my eyes shut, clutching the article and the map.

I need to look. Now. But I don't. I can't.

I try again, but my head drops, and my eyes remain shut.

Look up! Open your eyes, Lana. Look up, now!

I take a deep breath and quickly raise my head and open my eyes. I exhale.

The sign above the doorframe says, Le Café Dubois. It does exist.

But where is the line of hopefuls?

I move in closer and notice small square windows on the sides of the door. The windows are misty and stained with white paint. I peek in, but I can't see much of anything. I push my ear against the glass and manage to hear muffled voices and dishes clunking.

My heart beats fast, as I approach the door. I hold my breath, and with everything I've got, I push the heavy door with both hands. Red velvet curtains appear in front of me, exactly as Sylvia had described it.

I have arrived.

I walk through the curtains, and when it drapes down my back, a rush of excitement comes over me. I can't explain it.

The café is small. Dark wooden circle tables and chairs crowd the tight space. There are people standing by the windows, chatting and drinking, while a few are sitting by the bar. I scan the room and hope for a vacant spot. I see one in the back, but somehow, I can't get myself to move. My feet are glued to the tiled floor. What do I do now? I don't know how this all works. Do I seat myself or does someone seat me? Where is the matchmaker?

My heart is pounding. I continue to stand there as waiters briskly move past me with trays full of cups and saucers. Everyone is speaking in French, and I can't understand anything except for *"bonjour"* and *"s'il vous plaît"* and *"merci"*. My head is spinning. A breeze blows behind me, and the weight of the velvet curtains graze my back once more. A young woman enters all dressed up in a burgundy dress with a cream coat. She drifts past me and says something to one of the waiters then hurries to a vacant table by the bar, one I didn't even notice.

She lights up a cigarette and leans her elbows on the table, her eyes scouting the place, as if she is waiting for someone.

A few minutes pass, and I haven't moved. My eyes are fixed on the floor. When I look up, an old man enters the room from the kitchen. He is wearing black pants, a white button-down shirt, and a red apron.

My heart jumps.

Monsieur Francois Dubois?

It must be him.

He's shorter than I had imagined, his hair white as snow. His face is made up of deep-set eyes and a smile that appears permanent. He greets the patrons with a simple nod, and they respond with nervous smiles. He walks around the room with his hands behind his back, observing each customer, or shall I say, each hopeful. Meanwhile, I'm still hiding by the velvet curtains. I watch *Monsieur Dubois* approach a table by the cashier, where a lady is sitting alone. Her eyes light up, and she immediately acknowledges him and smiles. He offers his hand and she willingly takes it. He leads her to a table across the room where a young man sits alone. I can't see what he looks like from where I'm standing. *Monsieur Dubois* taps his table and the young man sits up and notices the lady now in front of him. He rises quickly and offers her a seat. *Monsieur Dubois* leans over and whispers something to them and they both laugh. He claps his hands together twice and spreads them and says *"Voilà,"* and leaves the couple. *Monsieur Dubois* walks around the room again and pauses a few feet away from where I'm standing. Our eyes meet. I freeze. Then he smiles at me.

Monsieur Dubois is smiling at me!

I smile back.

At least I think I did. I don't know. I'm too nervous. I unzip my purse and shove the map and the article inside. When I look up, the matchmaker is a few steps away from me.

My knees tremble. And I can't breathe.

In one swift motion, I turn around and exit the café and find myself sprinting down the alley.

What the hell am I doing? Where am I going?

I saw the matchmaker. The article is true. I witnessed him match two people right before my eyes. It was amazing.

But why did I leave?

Am I not ready to move on after all?

18

Cigarettes and Conversation

I make a wrong turn on the way back to my hotel.

I make a right instead of a left, and now I'm lost. Why did I rush out of the café? *Monsieur Dubois* was right there in front of me, but I choked at the last second and panicked. Why couldn't I go through with it?

I pick up my pace, as if I know where I'm going, but I have no clue, and I don't care anymore. A part of me wants to return to the café, but I'm too embarrassed to go back. Instead, I keep walking down a boulevard, across a bridge, and down an alley cursing at myself.

"Excusez-moi!" someone yells out. I pay no attention to it and maintain my speed. *"Excusez-moi, Madame!"* says the same voice, this time, louder and closer. But I ignore it.

Then I feel a light tap on my shoulder.

I stomp my feet, swinging around to face this person.

"What is it?" I blurt, in pure angst, refusing to look at the stranger now before me. "What do you want? Do you also have a love story you'd like to share with me? Another broken heart you'd like to dangle in front of me and make me feel sorry for you—another stranger I could care less about? Do you need to vent? Do you crave advice from someone who doesn't know you at all? What do you need from me? What about asking me about me for a change?" I rant, with my eyes fixed on the ground and my arms flailing in the air like an insane person.

I exhale slowly, lifting my head up.

A man is looking at me.

I get a glimpse of his face, and from my quick glance, he appears to be good looking. I swallow hard. My eyes drop down to the ground, avoiding his eyes. I panic inside wishing I could take back every word I had thrown at him.

Why of all times did I decide to blow up at the wrong time, at the wrong person?

"No broken heart here," he says, out of breath.

I detect a French accent.

"You dropped something," he says.

My whole face heats up, like someone had pulled my pants down in public. I want so much to look at this stranger whose husky voice has already lightened my mood, but I can't.

"I can't even look at you. I'm too embarrassed," I blurt, shaking my head.

"Please don't be embarrassed. I tripped trying to avoid dog shit while chasing after you," he says, with a laugh.

"Dog shit?" I repeat, with a short laugh, my nerves slowly relaxing.

"*Oui*, dog shit," he confirms.

How could anyone say such a line and make it sound so charming?

"That's embarrassing, but trust me, it doesn't beat what I just did," I reply, my eyes still planted on the ground.

"Why are you in such a hurry?" he asks.

"Oh, um, I was supposed to be somewhere, but I made a wrong turn, and well, now it's too late," I say, changing my story.

I lift my head slowly.

My cheeks heat up.

The man is beautiful.

"Let's get ice cream," he says and beckons me, his dark wavy hair blowing in the wind.

"Ice cream?" I repeat.

He smiles. *"Oui.* Ice cream."

"Umm, sure," I say, following him.

Am I really about to get ice cream with this stranger? *Oh no.*

It's happening.

It's the accent—his French accent!

The lady on the train said not to fall for the accent and the good looks. How do I say no, now? I can't say no, now. I can't do it. Who was that lady anyway, but a miserable stranger on a train? I don't have to listen to her. *Right?*

As we cross the street together, I take every opportunity to glance at him as often and as discreetly as I can. I watch this medium height man walking next to me, wearing a black wool coat, dark jeans and a pair of worn out gray boots and a cigarette in his left hand.

"Voilà," he announces.

But I'm too focused on getting a better look at him that I don't realize the ice cream shop is already in front of us.

He turns around, and my heart melts like ice cream on a hot summer's day. He's painfully gorgeous. His dark wavy hair drapes over his right eye. A scruffy light beard covers his chin and only makes him hotter. His lips are perfectly formed and his eyes are dark and intense. His woven beige scarf is carelessly wrapped around his neck, while his chest peeks through his white V-neck T-shirt.

I chuckle.

"Are you OK?" he asks, in his insanely hot voice.

"Well, it's pretty cold out here, and we're having ice cream," I say, imagining I'm running my fingers through his hair.

"Yes, but we still drink hot coffee in the summer, right?" he says.

"I guess," I say.

"Let's go?" he asks.

I nod and follow him inside.

"I don't know what to get," I say, staring at the overwhelming selection of flavors displayed on the wall. None of which I understand.

"Don't worry. I'll order for you," he says.

"Oh, thank you," I say.

I stand behind him as if I've never ordered ice cream in my life. I listen to him interact with the lady behind the counter. He pays, turns around with two cups of ice cream, and hands me one.

He holds the door as we exit. When the wind blows, I catch his scent. The kind of scent I wouldn't normally be attracted to, because there was the smell of cigarette mixed with a hint of cologne, but for some reason, today, it smells divine.

"What brings you to Paris?"

"How do you know I don't live here?"

"You're American."

"Sure, but I could still live here."

"You don't look like you do."

"There's a look to it?"

"Maybe."

"You're right. I don't live here."

"You gave up easily," he chuckles. "You could've lied," he teases.

"I'm a bad liar."

"That's good. Lying is bad," he says, smiling.

"Lying is bad," I repeat.

"Are you visiting for leisure or work?"

"Work," I answer. "I'm a writer."

He turns to me and nods. "You're a writer."

"I am. And what do you do?"

"I help with a family business."

"That's great."

"And I write, too."

"You do?"

He nods and pulls out a black Moleskine notebook from his coat pocket and shows me. Then he tucks it back inside.

"You handwrite everything?" I say, amused.

"*Oui*. What about you? How do you write?"

"I use my laptop." I glance at him. "You prefer a pen instead of a keyboard and a piece of paper instead of a screen."

"*Oui*."

"That's nice."

"My writing is not so good," he says, tossing his half-eaten ice cream cup in the trash.

"Why do you say that? Has anyone ever read them?"

"*Non,*" he replies. He pulls out a cigarette and offers me one. I shake my head. He lights it.

"I'd love to read them," I say.

He shakes his head, "No one reads my writing."

"But isn't that why you write? For it to be read by others?" I say, as we continue walking.

"Not for me," he says. "I write to say the things I won't or can't say to someone. I prefer no one reads them." He takes another drag of his cigarette as his wavy hair blows in the wind. He squints his eyes and exhales the smoke like he exhales his emotions on a piece of paper. He makes smoking look so damn sexy.

"Do you write in French?"

"Sometimes, but I write mostly in English."

"Maybe I can read them someday."

"Maybe," he says, smiling at me.

I look away and continue eating my ice cream. I no longer feel so cold.

19

The Café

Who is this mysterious guy next to me? Walking with me. Talking to me. I am floating away next to him, smiling and giggling at everything he says.

We stroll down a crowded street, our shoulders rub against each other, causing butterflies to flutter in my stomach. We stop at a café at the corner of Montparnasse and Rue Vavin.

"Hot coffee?" he asks, with a sly smile.

"Hot coffee," I say, smiling.

We enter and pass a row of small round tables and green wicker chairs. "Is this OK with you?" he asks, stopping at a table by the door.

"It's perfect," I reply.

A waiter wearing a white button-down, green vest, and black trousers stops and greets us. He promptly takes our order of two *café crèmes* and hurries off.

"Are you still in a rush?" he asks.

My lips part in an attempt to reply, but I pause, unsure of

how to respond. I had already forgotten about what had happened only hours ago.

"No, I'm not," I say, feeling my cheeks heat up.

He smiles.

We sit quietly, listening to the boulevard bustling with cars and people. When our order arrives, he tells me this is his favorite café, and how much he loves coming here to write. As we sip our coffee, he points out the characters who frequent the café. He tells me about the man with the round spectacles and the brown suit and says he always comes here in the morning to read the paper. Then there's the lady with the thick black hair and red lipstick, who meets with different people throughout the day, the café is her private office. Then there's the tall guy with the square face who always sits in the back and writes his novels. Then there's the old man with the sharp nose, a checkered suit, and a cane who sits in the middle of the café with his drawing book.

"He always draws the customers," he says.

"Do you think he's ever drawn you?" I ask.

He shrugs. "I don't know." He smiles. "But maybe he'll draw you."

When he says that, it reminds me of the artist on the train from Amsterdam.

"Actually," I say, shuffling through my purse, "an artist drew me on the train today." I reach inside and retrieve the folded piece of paper. "I had no idea he was drawing me until he left me this" I say, handing him my portrait.

He leans forward and unfolds the piece of paper. He looks at me, then the drawing, and smiles. "He captured you well," he says.

"He really did," I say, watching my stranger study my portrait.

"It's beautiful," he says, and hands it back to me.

"Thank you."

"What's the artist's name?" he asks.

"Philippe Renard," I answer.

"Ah, Philippe Renard," he says, nodding.

"You know him?" I ask, as I slip the drawing back inside my purse.

"Yes," he says. "He's my uncle."

I freeze up. "Oh my god! Are you serious?" I say, leaning forward.

He laughs. "No, I'm kidding."

I push him playfully.

"Why did you say that?" I say, now laughing.

"I just wanted to make you laugh," he says.

And he did.

20

The Perfect Stranger

After coffee, we resume our stroll until we arrive at Pont Neuf, overlooking the Seine River.

He stops on the sidewalk, pulls out another cigarette and lights it. He inhales and leans his arms on the stone bridge.

"I can never get tired of this view," he says, exhaling the smoke.

"I don't see how anyone can," I reply, admiring the calm water beneath the gray clouds.

"What do you write?" he asks.

I take a few steps forward. "I write a column for *Trend Magazine,*" I say, realizing I should have said *wrote* since I turned in my last article.

"What is it called?"

"*Trend Magazine,*" I reply.

He chuckles. "No, not the magazine, the column."

"Oh," I pause. "It's called 'Single and Loving It,'" I swallow hard.

"It sounds interesting," he says, and takes another drag of his cigarette.

"I guess," I shrug.

"Do you enjoy writing for the magazine?"

"I don't know. Sometimes I doubt if I'm even a writer." I laugh to myself. "Sometimes writing for my job takes the fun out of writing because most of the time, I don't like what I write. It feels like I have to force myself to feel a certain way in order to write something that I think my readers will want to read." I shrug "Or maybe it's the topic. Maybe I'm just tired of writing about being single."

"Are you single?" he asks, then stares out into the water.

I don't reply right away.

"Yes, I am," I finally say.

"Are you loving it?" he asks, jokingly.

"Absolutely," I say, laughing and shaking my head at the same time.

We share a laugh.

"Being single is not so bad, is it?"

"It has its moments," I say.

"I'm single, too," he says.

My heart leaps when he says that.

"And are you loving it?" Of course, I had to ask.

"It has its moments," he says, and winks at me and then takes another drag.

As I watch him blow the smoke up in the air, I wonder about what he's thinking. I watch his eyes squint, his lips move, and for the next few seconds, I imagine us together somewhere, doing something, doing anything. Then out of nowhere, I remember the magazine article and Le Café Dubois and the matchmaker.

Tomorrow is a big day for me.

It's when I'll meet my match.

And this man—this beautiful man standing next to me is merely a distraction, a stranger I will never see again after today.

"Writing can be hard sometimes," he says, interrupting my thoughts.

"Yes, it can be," I reply, clearing my throat.

I glance at him and he smiles, but instead of me smiling back, I babble. "Sometimes words have a life of their own. You simply rest your fingers on the keys and words appear on the blank screen in front you. Other times, they barely make it there," I say, leaning my elbows on the stone bridge, the breeze gently caressing my skin.

"Sometimes I hold the pen for hours, scribbling half sentences and then crossing them out. I sip my coffee and smoke my cigarettes until the day has turned into night, and I end up with nothing but broken lines made up of words that even I can't understand," he says, combing his hair with his hand.

"I know how that feels. A little too well," I say, shaking my head.

"But then other times, my coffee is left untouched, and I fill the pages quickly to the point where I don't even notice I have been sitting at the café for only a couple of hours, and yet, I have written so much."

"It comes and goes. We have good days and bad days." I pause, breathing in the cold air. "It feels different when I write for my column. It feels mostly contrived. But when I write about my own thoughts and feelings, I dive into a different world, and I am eager to get inside. At times, I have such a great time, I don't ever want to get out. Maybe I should publish those and not my column." I look down and watch the ripples in the water.

"It's different for me. When I write, I leave the words on the paper, and then I step away without looking back. I write to escape the feelings I can't deal with in real life."

"Hmmm," is all I could say.

"What are these other thoughts that you write about?" he asks.

"I don't know." I shrug. "They're random stuff about everything."

"Do you write these thoughts on your computer?" he asks.

"Yes. It's the only way I write."

"Pen and paper. The truth comes out naturally that way," he says.

"It's been years since I've written on paper. It seems archaic to do that now."

He looks away.

Did I offend him?

"I didn't mean, you. I was referring to writing on paper as being archaic," I say, embarrassed.

"It's OK," he says, and smiles.

He glances at his cigarette and pushes his hair away from his eyes, while the wind persistently blows it. I can smell his musky scent once more, and all it does is excite me.

"What do you write?" I ask, trying to distract myself from my thoughts.

He doesn't reply. Instead, he takes a few steps closer toward me. He lets the cigarette hang loosely in between his lips and grazes my cheek with the back of his hand. We stare into each other's eyes, like we're digging into each other's souls. Then he pulls the cigarette out of his mouth and slowly moves in. I start breathing heavily, and before I can make sense of what's happening, my eyes shut, and I feel his lips on mine. His warm mouth caressing mine, while his scruffy face tickles my skin. I kiss him back, and then a second too soon, I pull away.

Why did I pull away?

"I'm sorry," I say, shaking my head.

I've kissed a few men in my life, but nothing ever felt this good.

"What's wrong?" he asks softly, gazing into my eyes.

"I-I wasn't expecting that," I reply, fighting the urge to grab his face and kiss him again.

He takes a step back and says, "I thought kisses were supposed to be unexpected. Or they become less sweet."

And he's right. His kiss was sweet. Probably the sweetest kiss I've ever had in my life.

"I'm sorry, it's getting dark, and I-I," I say, stuttering, lost in the clouds, still high from our kiss.

"It's OK. You don't need to explain," he says.

"I have to go," I pause to clear my throat. "I have to be somewhere early tomorrow," I explain.

A part of me wants to tell him about why I came to Paris, but I hold back. He wouldn't understand. A silly American girl like me coming here to find a matchmaker in a café might sound a bit peculiar.

"I should go. I just arrived today, and I'm exhausted, and it's getting dark." I say, wishing I could take back every word.

"Of course. I understand," he says, with a smile.

"It was nice to meet you," I reply, walking backwards, regretting every step I take away from him.

He nods his head and smiles again.

I speed up, embarrassed and confused by my exit. A few steps later, I look back and notice him still there leaning against the stone bridge, watching me walk away. He takes one last drag and flicks his cigarette, while I turn around and fight hard to keep going the other direction.

21

Danielle and Cindy

I find my way back to the hotel.

I ring Danielle who conference calls Cindy.

"Are you seriously in Paris?" Danielle says.

"I am," I confirm smiling from ear to ear.

"What happened to Roy?" Cindy asks.

"I didn't go to dinner with him," I say, still smiling.

"That's my girl!" Cindy says.

"Wait, what made you change your mind?" Danielle asks, a bit skeptical.

"Well, I discovered why he left me," I explain.

"You did?" Danielle says.

"What is it?" Cindy asks.

"Roy cheated on me," I blurt out casually.

"What?" they say in chorus.

"That asshole," says the mother-to-be.

"When did he tell you?" asks the bride-to-be.

"He didn't. I ran into Dino, and he told me."

"Dino told you? I thought men had some code." Cindy says.

"I thought so, too," I reply.

"Eh, screw him. You left him and got your closure," Cindy says.

"So, what's going on in Paris?" Danielle asks.

"The café does exist," I announce, grinning.

"Oh my god, tell us what happened," Danielle says.

"Did you get matched? Who is he? How does he look?" Cindy asks.

"Let me know if it doesn't work out. I'll sign you up for Matchnow.com," Danielle says, jokingly.

"Nope, I didn't get matched. But no need to sign me up, Danielle," I say, with a chuckle.

"What do you mean? I thought you went to the café," Danielle says.

"I did." I shake my head. "But then I left."

"Oh, Lana," Danielle says, while Cindy argues with someone in the background.

"I'm sorry, I have to go. Apparently, my coordinator picked up the wrong favors. I swear I am going to fire her!" she says completely mortified, then hangs up.

"So, why did you choke?" Danielle asks, eager to hear my story.

"I don't know, I'm not sure. But trust me, it's OK," I assure her.

"Of course, it's OK, because you're going back tomorrow, right?"

"Yes," I say, spacing out, remembering the Parisian boy.

"Hello? Lana?" she says, noticing my long pause.

"I met someone." There, I said it. I couldn't hold it in any longer.

"What? Who? How?" she says, with a slew of questions.

"I met this guy. This mysterious guy," I say dreamily.

"When? Is he French?"

"Today, after I left the café." I pause. "Yes, he's French."

"How did you meet?"

"He followed me," I mumbled to myself.

"What do you mean he followed you?"

"It doesn't matter," I say, dismissing the details.

"Well, what's the problem?"

"I think I made a mistake," I blurt.

"What kind of mistake?"

"It was going great and all, and then he kissed me."

"He kissed you?" she says.

"Yes, he really did. He kissed me on the bridge, and it was amazing."

"OK, hold on a minute. You just described a scene from a movie," she says, shutting the refrigerator door.

"It did feel like a scene from a movie," I say, remembering the stranger's lips on mine. "That's exactly what happened. It was unexpected and perfect." I sigh. "But then I walked away."

"If it was perfect, why did you leave?"

"Because I'm going to the café tomorrow to meet my match, and I don't want to mess that up," I explain, realizing how foolish it all sounds now. How am I even sure about tomorrow?

"Lana, what if that was the guy for you? What if you let the right one, go?"

"I don't even know his name," I say, ignoring her comment. "I wish I knew his name," I mutter.

"Oh, Lana." She sighs. "I hope you find exactly what it is you're looking for."

"I guess I'll find out soon enough."

"Promise me you won't chicken out tomorrow. Go in there, find a table, and sit down," she instructs.

"I promise," I reply.

"Well, I need to go. I want a Big Mac."

"Go get your burger."

"Go get your man."

22

The Matchmaker

I wake up from a loud burst of laughter coming from the hallway. At first, it disturbs me. But when reality sinks in and I realize where I am, every nerve in my body relaxes.

I prop my pillows up against the headboard and lean back. Within minutes, the laughter from the hallway turns into footsteps that soon fade into silence, leaving me alone with my thoughts. I remember the Parisian boy and our kiss. All of a sudden, the memory of it all sends my heart racing, and I get antsy. I climb out of bed and begin pacing my cramped hotel room. And as I do, I obsess about what Danielle had said to me earlier.

What if I let the right one, go?

I mull over the thought, as I pull the curtain aside and look out the window. My jaw drops when I see what's behind it. From my tiny, narrow window, I could see a clear view of the Notre Dame Cathedral.

I stare at it in awe, as it shimmers against the dark skies. It reminds me of why I came to Paris.

I release the curtain and let the flimsy fabric cover the beautiful view. I crawl back into bed. It's 2:55 a.m. In a few hours, I'll be on my way to the café for another chance at finding love. But what if I don't get matched? What if the matchmaker decides not to pick me? What if I panic like I did yesterday and leave?

Before driving myself crazy with a thousand what-if's, I shut my eyes and force myself to think of happy thoughts. The first and only happy thought that comes to mind is the Parisian boy. Everything about him. Within minutes, I fall asleep.

The sun peeks inside my hotel room at around seven in the morning. As soon as I open eyes, a mix of emotions burst inside of me. I am anxious, nervous, terrified, but yet excited about today. I pull myself up and kick the sheets to the foot of the bed and hurry to the bathroom. I change into my black, long sleeve shift dress and put on some light makeup. I check my reflection in the bathroom mirror. I notice my hair is still damp, but it'll have to do, since I didn't bring a blow dryer, and the hotel doesn't provide one. I put on my red coat, grab my purse, and head to the lobby.

As I approach the front desk, I notice the giant clock hanging on the wall behind the concierge. It is 9:10 a.m.

"Bonjour, Madame," greets Josephine from behind the desk, the same lady who had checked me in.

"Bonjour," I greet back.

"Do you have an umbrella?" she asks.

"Oh, I didn't know it was raining," I reply.

"It's starting to rain now, and it's supposed to get heavier later."

"I guess I will need an umbrella," I say.

"We can lend you one," she says, and opens the closet door behind her. She pulls out a black umbrella with a wooden handle. "You can return it when you get back," she says, handing it to me. I thank her and exit the glass doors.

A couple of drops land on my forehead the moment I hit the sidewalk. A few steps later, it rains. The sound it makes when it lands on the pavement becomes music to my ears.

I used to wish I had Danielle and Cindy's lives. But now, I'm not sure I want what they have. Where I am now is different and exciting. I can't believe I'm walking on the cobblestone streets of Paris when just days ago, I was at the doctor's office, battling a psychosomatic stomachache.

My hands get cold and sweaty. I wipe them on the sides of my coat. Why am I more nervous today than I was yesterday?

The rain stops seconds after I glide past the Shakespeare and Company bookstore. I collapse my umbrella and commence my right turn at the end of the block. My heart races, and I keep going until the sounds of the city fade into silence.

I'm getting closer.

I pause to check my face in a side view mirror of a parked car and notice that my cheeks are rosy. I take a deep breath and proceed down the narrow alley. I increase my pace, until my eyes spot the café. I cross the street, holding my breath as I go over what Danielle had said to me.

Don't chicken out. Go in there, find a table, and sit down.

I exhale. I must do this now. This is my moment.

I take the last few steps and approach the red framed door. But when I get closer, my heart stops.

The door is shut.

It's padlocked.

Am I early?

I rattle the lock.

I search for a sign with the café hours, but instead, I find a piece of paper taped to the door. A note is written in black ink.

It says: Le café est fermé, mais l'amour vit sur.

What does this mean?

I need to know what this means.

I twist and turn searching for someone to translate it for me while digging inside my purse for a pen and paper. All I find is a napkin. I use it to write down the sentence and rush down the alley. There's a man walking his dog. I quickly approach him.

"Excuse me, do you speak English?" I ask, breathless.

He looks at me and stops. "A little," he says.

"Can you please translate this for me?" I beg.

He squints his eyes and says, "The café is closed, but the love lives on." Then he shrugs.

"Thank you. *Merci,*" I say.

He nods and walks away dragging his dog.

The café is closed, but the love lives on?

What does this mean? It doesn't make any sense. What is happening?

I storm back to the café and stand by the door, gaping at the note, struggling to make sense of it all. Then out of nowhere, I hear a woman's voice, *"C'est tres triste."*

I turn around and see a young lady in a brown coat crying.

"Are you OK?" I ask, wondering if she, too, had come to find her match but had lost her chance.

"It's very sad. Very, very sad," she says, her voice breaking. *"Monsieur Dubois* passed away early this morning," she explains.

My stomach drops. And in an instant, my world crumbles down ever so slowly.

"I'm sorry. W-what did you say?" I say, swallowing hard. "Are you sure?" I ask, with a giant lump in my throat.

"Yes, I'm sure. I worked at the café." She crouches down. "He is gone. *Monsieur Dubois* is gone," she says and takes off sobbing.

My mouth hangs open as I stand frozen on the sidewalk, my heart heavy, my mind whirling. I just saw the matchmaker yesterday, smiling at me. And now he's gone? I am such a fool. What was I thinking coming all the way to Paris expecting an old man I've never met to solve my problems? How could I have been so selfish?

I pick up my feet, forcing myself to leave the café, trudging away as fast as I can. I keep going until I end up at Notre Dame Cathedral. I approach an empty bench, and as soon as I sit down, I sob like a baby. My heart aches in places it never had before. I didn't even know the matchmaker, and yet, a great deal of sadness is bearing down on me. I lift my head up high trying to fight my tears back. I fix my eyes on the gray clouds hanging across the sky, hovering over me. I sit for a while, a long while, until I manage to control my tears. And then I pluck myself off the bench. Emotionally exhausted, I trudge down the cobblestone streets, making no plans other than to sulk. I'm trapped inside my thoughts, regretting this trip. Regretting everything.

It pours in spurts throughout the day, and for hours, I follow my feet to anywhere. I am somewhere, yet I am nowhere. Distraught. Still crying. Still hating myself. Still grieving. I dig through my purse with one hand trying to find something to wipe my eyes with, while the other hand clutches on to my loaned umbrella. All I find is the napkin I wrote on this morning, and I can't get myself to use it to wipe my tears, so instead, I cry again. I rush toward a corner and accidentally slam into someone. The handle of my umbrella slips off my hand, but I catch it before it hits the ground.

"Sorry," I say, my voice breaking, while I keep going, trying to stifle my cry.

"American, wait!"

My heart leaps.

I recognize the voice.

I hold my breath and turn around.

I gasp.

It's the Parisian boy from yesterday.

And for some reason, the sight of him makes me even more emotional that I begin to sob, louder, and I can't stop.

He runs to me and goes under my umbrella. I lift it up to accommodate him. His wet hair drips down his face as his dark eyes peer at me. He dries my tears with his fingers and stares at me, his hair soaked, his eyes red from the rain.

Why do we always meet when I'm the most vulnerable? His spontaneous affection overwhelms me but in a fantastic kind of way.

"Why are you crying?" he says, his forehead wrinkled.

Is he worried about me? But he doesn't even know me. I have no idea how to answer his question, so I say, "I heard some very sad news today," I explain. And just like that, I go back to crying.

"I'm sorry to hear that," he says, and cradles my face with his hands. Then he wraps his arms around me tight like we've known each other all our lives. I lean my head on his chest, and I could hear his heart beating as fast as mine.

When we release each other, he brushes his fingers through his wet hair.

"Where are you going now?" he asks, his eyes peering at me again.

"I don't know," I reply.

"Great. I'm going with you."

23

The Rain

Somewhere in the Latin Quarter, our hands meet, and I stop crying. His grip is firm but gentle. We walk briskly under the rain, like lovers escaping the world, rushing the streets painted with umbrellas—water splashing below our feet. My socks are soaked, but I don't care. I'm sad and happy all at the same time, and yet, it feels oddly perfect. This man means everything to me at this very moment. There is nothing else that matters. Not the rain, or the people, not the past or the present, and not even the fact that he's a stranger.

As we pass a crowd, he stops and looks at me. "You're all dressed up," he says. "We can't waste a pretty dress."

Then he takes my hand and leads me inside a small bistro on Rue Guisarde along Saint-Germain-des-Prés.

The place is cozy, the walls filled with old black and white photos of French musicians and movie stars. The tables are dressed with burgundy tablecloths and white paper. Wine glasses are set along with silverware and white porcelain plates. He asks for a table for two, and we get seated promptly in the corner next to two empty tables. No words from either one of us except for when we order our food. We eat in silence, exchanging glances like quiet conversations that only we could understand.

"You look beautiful," he says at the end of our meal.

"Thank you," I reply. "You, too," I say, wishing I had said something else. He smiles.

"Did you enjoy your food?" he asks.

"Yes, I did. Thanks," I reply, grabbing the napkin resting on my lap and proceeding to wipe my lips.

And then we are quiet again, but our lack of words doesn't mean we lack anything at all. The tension between us could break every window in the restaurant. His intensity burns through my skin. Once in a while, he would glance at me, as if telling me a story with his eyes. He brushes back his damp hair with his fingers, and his eyes come to perfect view. His soul almost becomes visible, and yet, I can't see right through him.

When our dinner ends, we hurry toward the door. He takes the umbrella from me and holds it.

"Let's run," he says, his eyes glowing.

"Let's run," I repeat, and we exit the restaurant.

Our hands clasp together, and it feels as though I have walked into a dream. Here I am with this beautiful man, pushing through the cramped streets of Paris. This cannot be real.

Minutes later, he pulls me into a bar. The place is long and narrow, dark, and dingy. Alcohol, smoke, and sweat fill the room. We sit down at the bar, next to a row of empty wooden stools.

"Would you like a drink?" he asks.

"Sure."

"Anything in particular?"

"No," I reply. I can't think of anything right now—not a name of a drink, not even my own name. I am trying my best to fathom this movie that I am starring in. My lines I have never seen. I have nothing memorized. Whatever happens, I hope this movie never ends.

He orders our drinks and lights another cigarette. Minutes later, two shot glasses appear in front of us.

He rests his cigarette on an ashtray and whispers to me. "This should relax your nerves."

"I hope so."

We face each other, lift our glasses and chug our drinks down. The heat burns my throat and drops down to my chest.

"Wow," I say.

"It's strong," he says.

"Very strong."

As I recover from the drink, I wonder what he's thinking. He is different today. But then again, I don't know him at all. I gaze at him, watching his eyes in perfect contemplation.

"I'm glad you're here," he says, his hand still wrapped around his empty shot glass.

"I'm glad you're here," I say with a smile, realizing how being with him has made me forget how sad and upset I was, and still am. "I'm sorry you had to see me like that. The last thing I ever wanted was for anyone—especially you, to see me crying." I pause, as a clear vision of the café rushes through my mind.

"Don't be sorry. We all cry sometimes."

I smile. "But thanks to you and the alcohol, I'm better now" I say, with a smile.

He winks at me and turns around to say something to the bartender, and seconds later, two shot glasses filled to the rim appear before us.

I laugh. "Are we doing this again?"

He grabs a shot glass and pushes the other one closer to me. I shake my head and whisk it up and chug it down fast. I slam the glass on the table.

"That burns so deep."

He smiles at me as a strange feeling rushes through my veins, invigorating me.

He grabs my hand and says, "Let's go."

We exit the bar unto a busy street. It's dark and loud and wet. We rush off, embracing the rain, passing people from every direction, moving fast, as though we are chasing time.

We dash through the sidewalks and streets, splashing through puddles of water, and my heart dances to the beat of the rain hitting the pavement. He leads me to a corner and runs his fingers through my wet hair, pushing them away from my face. His comfortable gestures baffle me, but what baffles me even more, is how easily I have welcomed them.

"My name is Jean-Luc," he says.

"Jean-Luc," I repeat.

He smiles at me.

"I'm Lana," I say.

"Lana," he repeats.

I lift my head up to the sky and shut my eyes for a second, pretending that each raindrop is a little kiss from Eros. When my eyes open, Jean-Luc is still smiling at me. He takes my hand again, and we disappear into a sea of people.

Minutes later, we enter Café de Flore on Saint-Germain-des-Prés.

"Coffee?" he asks, leading us along a tight aisle between crowded tables and chairs.

"Sure," I reply, squeezing through with our wet clothes dripping.

We park ourselves at an empty table toward the back. Jean-Luc flags the waiter and orders. Everything moves fast, and we're moving right along with it. A waiter dressed in black and white swerves in between people and tables and delivers our drinks. We sip, talk, laugh and do it all over.

Maybe it's the rain or the drinks or being in Paris or being in Paris with Jean-Luc, or all of the above, but something feels different inside of me. As we sit here, I am in a complete frenzy. I am excited about every little thing, as if it were the first time I have ever tasted coffee or have been inside a café. My heart is beating at an unusual speed, and there's a giant smile painted on my face, and I don't know how to get rid of it. I don't want to get rid of it.

For the first time in a long time, I am happy.

I am absolutely happy.

We finish our drinks and order more. Amidst the noise, we converse, and I become more alive and exhilarated than I was the first time we walked in. How do I hold on to this feeling a while longer?

People continue to filter in and out as Jean-Luc and I keep ordering. After our fifth cup, he looks at me and says, "I don't want to go home today."

"I don't either," I say, fiddling with my cup.

"Let's not go home," he says.

"Let's not."

"What do we do now?" I say, leaning forward.

"We walk some more," he says.

"Where do we go?"

"It doesn't matter. It's Paris."

We pay our bill and head for the door.

A church bell rings as we exit the café. It's midnight. The cold wind picks up, and minutes later, the rain pours hard on us. Jean-Luc holds the umbrella and puts his arm around me, keeping me as close to him as possible. It's cold and wet, and I have no idea where we are. But I don't care. Being here is better than being anywhere else.

After a long and beautiful stroll in the rain, we end up at an apartment building. We enter a courtyard where even late at night, you could see the giant potted plants and the beautiful trees. We ascend the stairs and land on the second floor. We continue down a dark hallway with paint chipping off the walls. Jean-Luc pulls out a set of keys from his coat pocket and unlocks the first door to the right.

"I live here," he says.

"I thought you didn't want to go home."

"I didn't. But it's too cold out there, and we need to rest."

I swallow hard.

He pushes the door open, and I enter without any hesitation.

The first thing I see is the kitchen, and to its right, is the living room. Across the living room is a bedroom with a doorframe but no door. I head to the living room.

"I'll be back," he says, and disappears into the bedroom. Seconds later, he comes out with a towel and a black T-shirt and hands them to me, as my entire body shivers.

"You can use the bathroom behind you," he suggests.

"Thanks," I reply, still unable to grasp today's events.

I leave the umbrella in the tub and wash off the makeup smeared all over my eyes. I dry my head with the towel and run my fingers through my damp hair. I change into the T-shirt he gave me and hang my dress and coat by the shower. I saunter back into the living room. Jean-Luc has already changed. He's wearing a gray V-neck T-shirt and comfortable pants. He stands in the living room, flipping through vinyl records and turns around when he notices me.

He glances at me and then at the records. "Do you mind if I play some music?" he says, in a low tone.

"No, not at all. Please do," I say, curious to hear what he would play.

Soon the sound of rain tapping against the windows dissipates and is replaced by an electric guitar slowly filling the room and wildly strumming my heart.

"Do you know this song?" he asks.

"No, I don't."

"It's called 'Wish You Were Here' by Pink Floyd," he says.

He smiles, drags his bare feet on the parquet floor toward me and takes my hand.

I follow him into his bedroom where it's dim and cozy. His bed leans against a bare wall. Books are scattered on the floor and a lamp with a light that flickers sits on his side table. He lies on the bed and gently pulls me by the hand to join him.

What am I doing here?

I follow his lead and lie with my back facing him, my body trembling. He lays the sheets over us and pulls me closer, his arms around my waist. He rests his chin on my shoulder, his warm breath caressing my hair.

And just like that, I get comfortable in the arms of a stranger.

24

Secret

My eyes snap open.

It's dark. I lift my head and catch a glimpse of Jean-Luc sitting on the floor, his back leaning against the foot of the bed. He has a cigarette in one hand and a book on the other. A candle is lit inside a clear glass jar on top of his dresser. In a world where computers and smart phones are necessities, here is a man who still believes in notebooks and pens and candles and books. He is old fashioned and mysterious, which are the very reasons why I am drawn to him.

Jean-Luc takes a deep drag, flips a page of his book, and exhales. The smoke hangs in midair for a second like a ghost flashing through. In my usual world, I would've despised the sight and the smell of his cigarette. But this is not my usual world, and this is not my usual self. Instead, the smoke becomes a magical sight and even the smell captivates me.

I raise my head higher to get a clearer view of Jean-Luc. As I watch him and listen to the rain dancing on his windowpane, realizing I am in a stranger's home with no clue of who he is, and yet, I am not afraid. Fear has not crossed my mind—not even for a second. I remain still and quiet, fascinated by his silhouette moving in the dark, his head shifting left to right as he scans the pages of the book.

His body turns to his left, enough that I can see him take another drag of his cigarette. He squints his eyes and buries the last of it into an ashtray already full of ashes. He licks his lips and rests the book on the floor. I lower my head and shut my eyes as I sense him glance at my direction. I hear him get up and walk out of the room. The refrigerator door opens and shuts, and I hear liquid poured into a glass. Jean-Luc returns. I crack my eyes open and see him rest a glass of water on the floor and then sits down. He picks up a different book, this one thicker than the last. He flips through the pages, reading off lines, whispering them quickly and quietly. I wonder if he does this nightly, or if for some reason tonight, he cannot sleep. A part of me wants to let him know that I am awake, but find it too irresistible and alluring to watch him instead in silence. There is something intriguing and comforting about observing his every move in the dark and listening to his quiet murmurs of words and phrases. Everything he says sounds like poetry.

My eyelids fold, but I keep fighting to keep them open. I want to see more of him, but my body fights back, and I doze off. Soon, I wake up again. Jean-Luc is still on the floor with the candle now next to him. The candle is shorter, the wicker close to the end. He is holding a piece of paper and a pen, writing vigorously, as if the words will run away if he does not jot them down. What could he be writing? He rises, holding sheets of papers in his hands. He opens the top drawer of his dresser and stores his writings and shuts it slowly. He leaves the room, and I hear him wash up in the bathroom. A few minutes later, he comes back. I peek to see him with my eyes half-open. He bends over, picks up the candle from the floor, and places it on the dresser. I shut my eyes.

He climbs up on the bed and arranges the sheets on top of me, his warm breath on my forehead, sending shivers down my spine. I hold my breath, trying to slow down my heartbeat. Even now, I still don't want him to know I am awake. He lies down, as I continue to face away from him. A few seconds later, my eyelids open. Now, I can't sleep. All of a sudden, I remember the matchmaker. My heart aches, as the memory of him smiling at me flashes through my mind. I close my eyes and reopen them, hoping to shake off my sadness, but it doesn't work. I stare at the ceiling until the light on the candle fades. Then I slowly turn to face Jean-Luc who is fast asleep, breathing quietly. I watch him until I get lost into a trance.

Watching him tonight will be my little secret.

25

The Apartment

I wake up in Jean-Luc's bed, his sheets covering my bare legs. Last night was amazing and memorable. More memorable and more amazing than any other time I've ever had with a man. Something about Jean-Luc enthralls me. Catching him awake last night and secretly watching him has piqued my curiosity, that now I yearn for even more. All we did was lay here, but somehow, it felt greater than that.

I turn to my side and notice the empty space next to me. A second later, Jean-Luc enters the room with a cup in each hand, his hair wet and brushed back, revealing his handsome face.

"Bonjour," he greets, his voice muffled by the cigarette in his mouth. He's wearing a white T-shirt, a black cardigan, gray skinny jeans, and black ankle boots.

I sit up, pull the sheets off, my bare legs now exposed. I ignore it and scoot to the side of the bed with only my borrowed T-shirt on.

Jean-Luc sits down beside me.

"Bonjour," I greet, in my heavy American accent.

"What time is it?"

He hands me a cup.

"Time for coffee," he says.

I take the cup and smile.

"It's eight," he says.

"It's early," I reply.

He watches me stare into my cup.

"It's espresso," he says.

I laugh. "Oh, I know." I inhale deeply. "Forgive me, I'm in a bit of a shock right now." I pause, looking around.

"I still can't believe I'm in Paris, let alone, sitting here on your bed… with you," I explain, avoiding his eyes by taking a sip.

"I'm happy you're here," he says.

I glance up at him and say, "I'm happy I'm here, too."

I take another sip, savoring the bitter taste of coffee in my tongue.

He smiles and takes a drag of his cigarette and blows the smoke toward the empty doorframe.

My eyes land on the books scattered on the floor. It reminds me of my little secret—Jean-Luc reading off lines and writing in the dark, and for a moment, I almost ask him what books he read or what he wrote last night. But I catch myself and remember that he didn't know I was awake, so I let the thought pass.

"Are you hungry? There's a baguette on the counter and some fruit. There's also cheese and jam in the fridge," he says.

"I'm fine right now. Thanks," I say.

He glares at his watch, scratches his chin lightly, and gets up.

"Are you going somewhere?" I ask, hoping he'd say no.

"I am," he says, exhaling. "I wish I didn't have to. I'm sorry," he says, walking out of the bedroom. "I have to go, but I'll be back in a few hours. You're welcome to stay, or go. Whichever you prefer," he says, his face a bit frazzled.

I feign a smile, hiding my disappointment.

"I'll go back to my hotel," I say, getting up and glancing at my borrowed top.

"I'll take you there," he says.

"Great. I'll be ready in five minutes," I say, following him to the living room.

"*D'accord,*" he says.

"Pardon?"

"I'm sorry." He smiles. "*D'accord* means OK."

"OK."

We chuckle then he turns around to grab his coat while I hurry to the bathroom.

We share a cab to my hotel. When we arrive, Jean-Luc walks me to the door.

"May I see you tonight?" he asks.

I smile, relieved that he wants to see me again.

"*D'accord,*" I say, hoping I pronounced the word correctly.

He smiles then cups my shoulders tightly. "I will meet you here at seven," he says.

"Seven sounds good," I confirm. I want to ask him where he's going in such a hurry, but it isn't right for me to pry. After all, we've only just met.

When Jean-Luc hops back in the cab, I turn around and push the door open. I stop by the front desk to return the umbrella and ascend the dreary staircase.

It's been an hour since I entered my hotel room. I've showered and changed, and now I'm sitting on the hotel bed, listening to the old springs creaking inside the mattress. I get up, walk to the window, and gaze out at the Notre Dame Cathedral. In an instant, the vivid memory of the matchmaker walking toward me and smiling repeats in my head, followed by the memory of the closed café and the lady sobbing. My chest tightens and tears build up fast. Desperate for fresh air, I leave the hotel.

Minutes later, I come across a small flower shop next to a *pâtisserie*, a few blocks away from where I'm staying. I decide to purchase a bouquet of white flowers and head back to the place I had come to Paris for. As I approach the café, my body weakens. I know it's a terrible idea to go back, but I keep going anyway. My eyes fog up. When my tears hit my cheeks, and my vision clears, I gasp at the sight before me. Flowers and signs and cards scatter in front of the café. But no one is around except me. With my hands trembling, I place the flowers in a vacant spot by the door, and as I do so, I can't help but scan the cards and notes. The abundance of love and gratitude for the late *Monsieur Dubois* overwhelms me that my body shakes. In an absurd way, this all feels too close to my heart. As though I had known the matchmaker, and not known him a little bit, but known him like a dear friend or a close relative. I take a deep breath, and as I exhale, tears pour in a fluid motion. When I calm myself down, I proceed along the narrow alley one last time. In no hurry, I

make my way back to the hotel, with my head down low,
and my heart still hurting.

26

Eiffel Tower

The hotel phone rings the minute I enter my room. It's the concierge calling. Someone is waiting for me downstairs. I check the time. It's a little after five. It must be Jean-Luc. He's two hours early.

I hurry downstairs and notice him first, sitting on one of the chairs in the lobby. When I get closer, he sees me and immediately gets up, and we rush toward each other.

"I'm glad you're early," I say, falling into his arms.

"I'm glad, too," he says. "I thought maybe you'd want to see more of Paris."

"I really do."

"What do you want to see first?" he says.

"The Eiffel Tower," I announce, a bit too quickly. "Are you OK with that?" I ask, wishing now that I had picked a different sight. Perhaps one that was less predictable.

"*Bien sûr,*" he says, and puts his arm around me, and we exit the hotel.

We catch a cab to Place du Trocadéro, where we blend in with a flock of tourists marveling at the breathtaking view of the Eiffel Tower.

"It's magnificent," I say, staring up at it in awe. "Pinch me," I say to Jean-Luc, but he kisses me instead. Then he takes my hand, and we make our way through the crowd of tourists and souvenir peddlers. We walk past statues and fountains, a garden, and soon, a beautiful carousel. The closer we get to the Eiffel Tower, the more I can't take my eyes off of it.

"Would you like to go up?" Jean-Luc asks, after we arrive at the grand structure.

"Absolutely," I say, wrapping my arms around his.

We walk under the tower and join a long line of tourists waiting for the lifts. But about ten minutes later, we change our minds and decide to challenge ourselves by taking the stairs. As we make our way up to the first level, my thighs start to burn. By the time we get to the top of the second level, my knees are shaking. I try to say something, but I am too out of breath to speak. Jean-Luc tries to say something, too, but he is also unable to speak.

When our eyes meet, we burst into laughter.

"Maybe we should've waited for the lift," I say, both of us still laughing.

Minutes later, we finally make it to the top.

"*Voilà.* So, what do you think?" Jean-Luc asks.

I gaze down at the picturesque view of the city below. "Amazing."

"Was it worth the climb up?"

"Definitely."

We check out the view from different corners, while Jean-Luc points out some of the popular sights of the city.

"I'd like to take you somewhere else now," he says.

"Where?"

"You'll see."

We take the lift down this time and catch a cab to Champ de Mars. A few minutes later, we arrive at the Luxembourg Gardens in the Sixth Arrondissement. We walk past empty green metal chairs scattered across the gardens and cross a maze of trees. I glance at Jean-Luc and notice his eyes deep in thought.

"It's lovely here," I say, breaking the silence.
Jean-Luc smiles. Then he looks at the trees, and a gloomy gaze lingers in his eyes.

"Can I ask you something?" I say.

"Sure."

"How did you find me yesterday?"

"La magie," he says.

"Magic?" I say, taking a guess.

"Oui," he replies, staring at the sky.

"Magic," I repeat, satisfied with his answer.

We stay quiet for a while, comfortable with our silence. I look out at the garden admiring the colorful flowers and the beautiful water basins.

"You puzzle me," I say, surprised by the words that leave my mouth.

"What do you mean?" he says, glancing at me, his eyes full of wonder.

"I don't know. You have a mystery about you that I can't seem to put my hands on."

"Maybe you have a mystery about you that I can't put my hands on."

I shake my head. "No, I don't think I'm mysterious." I look at him. "Don't get me wrong, I like that I find you mysterious. It keeps me on my toes."

"It's a good thing?" he says.

I chuckle. "Yes, it is."

He lights up a cigarette, his eyes focused on a row of trees.

"I wrote for the first time here," he says.

"Right here?" I ask, referring to our current spot.

We pause somewhere in the middle.

"Well, not right here, but it was under one of these trees. I remember hiding somewhere here," he says, looking around. "I craved my solitude that day. I didn't want to talk to anyone. I didn't want anyone to know how I was feeling. And so, I wrote."

"How old were you?"

"I was twelve." He puts the cigarette back in his mouth and inhales slowly then blows the smoke up in the air. "How old were you when you first began writing?"

"Fifteen or sixteen."

"What did you write about?" he asks.

"About my first broken heart," I laugh to myself. "I wrote four to five pages in my diary in one night. I don't remember much about what I wrote. But what I do remember was feeling quite relieved after I finished writing."

"*Ah, oui.*" He nods. "Sometimes writing can be healing. Some kind of remedy," he says.

Some kind of remedy. I like that.

"What about you? Did you write about your first broken heart, too?"

"Something like that," he says, looking away.

"Do you remember what you wrote?"

He squints his eyes and nods. "I do. I remember I wrote a few lines," he says.

"A few lines," I repeat, facing him. "What were they?"

He turns to me and finds my wide eyes staring at him.

"Do you really want to hear them?"

"Yes, I do."

He inhales again, blows the smoke, and says, "I wrote: *I am bluer than the sky, my heart is paler than the clouds, I apologize for my distant heart, but I don't believe in love.*"

"Twelve? You wrote that at twelve years old?"

"Twelve," he confirms. "I will never forget it."

"It's beautiful," I say.

"Merci."

"So, you're a poet," I say.

"A poet?" he repeats then shrugs. "Maybe so."

"That was deep and intense. She must have been some girl," I say, hoping to get more information.

He rubs his cheek. "I wish it were about some girl, it probably would've been easier to get over. But it wasn't," he says.

"It wasn't?"

"No." His eyes narrow. "I wrote the poem because of my parents," he says.

"Oh," I reply, not expecting to hear that.

"I was born in Paris. When I was about two, my father's job moved us to London. When I was eight, he took me aside one night and told me that he might not see me for a while. I didn't know what he meant. When I woke up the next morning, he was gone. I didn't know then that he had left for good. I was a child, and I didn't understand what was going on. I used to ask my mother about my father, but every time I did, she would change the subject." He shrugs. "Eventually, I gave up asking."

My heart feels heavy for him.

"I'm sorry to hear that," I say, now regretting sharing my silly story about my diary and about some boy who never meant anything to me.

"A few months following my father's sudden departure, my mother and I moved back to Paris to live with her family. Four years later, she took me aside," he pauses to clear his throat, "and said she had to go somewhere for a while. The day I wrote that poem was a week after she left. A week after I realized I would never see her again."

How could his parents do such a thing? How could anyone leave their child? All I want to do right now is hold him in my arms and be here for him. I gaze at Jean-Luc, and at that moment, his pain was mine. Through his eyes, I could see how bruised his heart still is.

"I'm so sorry, Jean-Luc. I can only imagine what you've been through. I would have been devastated."

"I was devastated and hurt and confused. I was very young, and I didn't know how to deal with it. I was abandoned by both of my parents for reasons I will never know. For years, I believed that something had to be wrong with me because I sent my own parents away. I blamed myself for a long time and even hated myself. It took me a while to realize it had nothing to do with me, that whatever their reasons for leaving me was for them, not for me."

I didn't say a word. Instead, I held his hand, hoping my little gesture would comfort him.

"About five years ago, I found out that my father had passed away."

"Oh, Jean-Luc, I'm so sorry to hear that," I say, squeezing his hand.

He tightens his lips. "But when I found out, I didn't feel anything. Not sorrow or anger. Nothing." He inhales slowly. "My heart was empty for him. I wasn't capable of feeling anything anymore."

He shrugs his shoulders and takes another hit and blows the smoke up in the air. *"C'est la vie,* right?" he says, with pain in his eyes.

I could see it wasn't an easy subject, and it took a lot for him to admit it to me—a stranger he had only met.

"I have many scars, Lana," he says, gazing away. "Do you still want to be with me?"

I move in closer. "Oh, Jean-Luc. Of course, I still want to be with you. Don't you know we all have scars?" I lean my head on his shoulder, and he squeezes my hand.

We resume our stroll and head toward the water basin, pausing behind the green metal chairs.

A drop from the sky lands on my head. I look up and see a thick blanket of dark clouds.

"It's about to rain," I say, brushing my hand on my head.

Jean-Luc sticks his hand out and catches a couple of drops. We smile at each other and don't bother to move. Within minutes, it rains, and in seconds, it pours. Everyone around us scampers away, and soon, we are left alone in the garden, still in the same position.

"How about a stroll?" he says, extending his hand out to me.

"I'd love that," I reply, placing my hand on his.

Jean-Luc and I saunter away as if it were the first day of summer. Our shoes squishing against the wet grass, but we proceed as if our feet are touching warm sand on a beach on a beautiful sunny day. Our slippery hands remain clasped together, our clothes drenched, and our bodies cold. All I can see are a sea of blurry faces. The only clear face is that of Jean-Luc's.

We walk on the sidewalks, slow and steady, down alleyways, and soon arrive at his apartment building. We ascend the stairs, our clothes soaked, and for the first time, we let go of each other's hands. Jean-Luc reaches for his keys and opens the door. He walks in, and I follow. As the door shuts behind me, my stomach crowds with butterflies, and I breathe heavily. Jean-Luc peels off his coat, his sweater, kicks off his shoes by the door and slips inside his bedroom. I pause in front of the bathroom, my knees shaking.

He looks back at me affectionately.

"I-I should probably go," I blurt out nervously, my dress clinging to my body, and my shoes dripping on his floor. He approaches me with a wondering look.

"Why are you leaving?" he asks.

"I-I need to change my clothes," I explain, my voice trembling.

Why am I so nervous? And why am I talking about leaving, when every part of me wants nothing more than to be with him?

I don't need to be anywhere else.

"You can borrow another shirt," he says.

"You want me to stay?" I ask, my heart pounding in my chest.

Jean-Luc approaches me. My knees shake even more. I quickly adjust my feet, struggling to stand still. He touches my wet hair, and a cold shiver shoots down my spine.

"I'll get you a towel," he says, in a low tone.

I nod.

But he doesn't get me a towel. Instead, he gently cradles my face with his hands, gazes into my eyes and kisses my open mouth. Then he kisses my cheek, then my neck, and I freeze. His soft lips caress mine again, and I kiss him back, feeling his tongue slowly entering my mouth. My tongue meets his, and I kiss him like I've never kissed anyone before. He releases me and takes off his wet T-shirt, pulling it from the back revealing his slender body. He takes my hand and leads me into the bedroom. He kisses me again in the dark, pulling me closer with his hands on the small of my back. A hundred shivers run down my spine. He lays me on the bed slowly, his weight now on top of me. I close my eyes, as his scent instantly drugs me and awakens every ounce of bliss hiding inside of me. He lifts my dress, taking his time, rolling up the fabric with his fingers. He glances up at me and climbs my body with his warm lips on my cold skin.

And I slowly lose my mind.

27

Bliss

We fell asleep around two or three in the morning.

Maybe. I don't know for sure. All I remember is the rain tapping on the window, creating a soothing sound that lulls us to sleep.

When the rain stops, the silence awakens me. It's dark. My head is on Jean-Luc's bare chest and his head is leaning on mine. I gently push my cheek against his chest. He moves a little, but only to pull me closer. As I listen to his heartbeat, I can't help but wonder how I got here. I've never done anything like this before. I've never slept with a guy I hardly knew, especially not after only two days of knowing him. I've never had a one-night-stand, and even if I had, I could never compare this to that or to anything else for that matter.

When my eyes adjust to the darkness, I tilt my head back slightly to look at Jean-Luc. His light beard brushes up against my forehead. I stare at his lips in the dark. His beautiful full lips. Every bit of me wants to kiss him, but

I don't, because I don't want to wake him up, so I tilt my head back down, but when I do, his fingertips slowly lift my chin. Even in the dark, I could tell his eyes are looking at me. In seconds, his mouth touches mine, and with no hesitation, I turn to my stomach and find myself on top of him, kissing him hard, his one hand on my nape, the other on the small of my back. Our naked bodies collapse unto each other as the sheets slip off the bed.

It's been a long time since I've slept this well. Did I dream anything at all? I don't know. It doesn't matter. My reality is a dream.

"Are you up?" he whispers.

I crack one eye open. Jean-Luc is already dressed in a gray V-neck shirt and blue jeans. He sits on the bed.

"Yes, I'm awake" I reply, combing my hair with my fingers and pulling myself up.

"Bonjour," he greets, with a smile.

"Bonjour," I greet back. "When did you get up?"

"An hour ago." He leans over and kisses me. "When you're ready, let's get breakfast."

"Sounds good," I reply, sitting up.

He turns away, and as I watch him leave the room, I let my head fall back on the pillow. I look around and notice my dress still draped over his side table, exactly how we left it last night. My one shoe is in his bedroom. I'm not sure where the other one ended up. I turn my head to the right. My eyes settle on the window. I put on one of Jean-Luc's T-shirts from the bed, rush to the window, and push the curtains aside. I gasp at the view, as if I've never seen rooftops in my life. My forehead presses against the glass, and I watch the rain dance on the zinc rooftops, glistening beautifully. My eyes wander off to every white frame window across the way, wishing I could peek inside each home and take a quick glimpse of each life and each story. It makes me curious and gives me an itch to write. I've always liked the rain, but never like this. This is different.

Soon, I hear music coming from the living room. Piano keys softly playing followed by a beautiful woman's voice singing in French. Although I don't understand a single word, I am drawn to the melody and to her soothing tone. I leave the bedroom and notice my other shoe in a magazine rack. Jean-Luc is standing by his vinyl records, flipping through them. His face lights up when he sees me and extends his arm out. I slide across the room barefooted and meet his hand with mine. He pulls me in closer.

"Do you know this song?" he asks.

I shake my head.

"'*Parlez moi d'amour*' by Lucienne Boyer," he says.

"What does it mean?"

"It means, 'Tell me about love,'" he explains.

"It's lovely."

When the song ends, he plays it again and wraps his arms around me, and I wrap my arms around him. We stand there holding each other, swaying back and forth until the song fades. Then I excuse myself to shower and change.

We leave his apartment and pick up fresh baguettes and coffee from a bakery a few blocks away from his place. We bring our breakfast to a small park close by, where we find an empty bench. Jean-Luc wipes it with a napkin before we sit down. It's cold and crisp out, the sky, a light shade of gray and blue. As I sip my coffee, a woman walks by talking on her phone, while eating a fresh baguette. Another woman whisks by on her bike with a baguette sticking out of her purse. An old couple holds hands as they cross the street, while a young couple steals a kiss in the corner. Everything is like a clip from a movie that I have seen many times before.

I glance at Jean-Luc, his beard fuller today. He looks different from the first day I met him but just as handsome. I gaze back at the street, slowly soaking in the sights and the sounds of the city.

I am in Paris.

And I don't ever want to leave.

28

Montmartre

"I wish I had my phone," I say, digging inside my pockets.

Jean-Luc and I are standing at the bottom of the stairway on Rue Foyatier in the Eighteenth Arrondissement.

"Why? Do you need to call someone?" he asks, concerned.

"No, I want to use it to take pictures," I say, with a chuckle.

"Technology," he says, shaking his head.

We share a laugh.

"Too bad, I don't have it," I say, disappointed.

"I'm sorry," he says.

"I guess I'll just have to remember everything," I say with a shrug.

"You will," she says, winking.

We ascend the steps passing trees and beautiful lampposts. I can't help but wish we could come back at night to see them all lit up.

"I used to run up these steps when I was a child," Jean-Luc says, stopping ahead of me and looking down.

"How fast were you?" I say, taking a couple of steps ahead of him.

"I was fast," he says proudly.

"I'll race you," I say.

Jean-Luc looks up at me, his eyes glowing. He grins and yells, "Go!"

He charges up the steps passing me, and I take off running as fast as I could and pass him. When I make it to the top, I raise my arms up in the air, as though I had won something. And maybe I have. Because when Jean-Luc makes it to the top, it feels like I got my prize.

"I let you win," he jokes, catching his breath.

"Sure, you did," I say, squinting my eyes at him.

As we resume, Jean-Luc pauses and says, "You're lucky today."

"That wasn't luck. I won fair and square," I say, my hands now on my waist.

"No, not that." Jean-Luc cups my shoulders and turns me around and says, "Look. No fog."

"Oh." I take a deep breath. "Wow."

I stare at the magnificent view of Paris, as Paris stares back at us. "You're right," I utter softly. "I am lucky," I say, resting my head on his shoulder. Jean-Luc puts his arm around me.

Minutes later, our feet lead us to Place du Tertre where tourists gather amongst the artists, waiting for their portraits to be painted or drawn. We swerve through the crowded square and eventually find ourselves passing a windmill and a beautiful street with amazing houses covered with ivy.

"This is breathtaking," I say, stopping in the corner of Rue des Saules. "I would love to see what this house looks like inside. Wouldn't you?" I say, admiring an elegant gray three-story house with thick ivy framing the windows.

"Yes, I would," he says, smiling at me. "You'll see more houses like this as we go on."

"I can't wait," I say, wrapping my arm around his.

We proceed up the hill, and just as Jean-Luc had said, we see more houses covered in ivy, one more beautiful than the next. And then somewhere down a steep hill, he shows me the secret vineyard of Paris.

"This is why I should've brought my phone, or a camera," I say, gazing at the beautiful hill covered with vines.

"Let's come back here soon," I say.

"Let's do that," he says, squeezing my hand.

We continue our tour of Montmartre, walking along a row of souvenir shops and fabric stores. We even stop at a wall covered with "I love you" written in different languages. We read as many as we can out loud until our necks grow sore from looking up.

I thought it was impossible for me to love this city any more than I already do. But taking this stroll with Jean-Luc up and down the hills of Montmartre has made me realize I have so much more to see. And I can't wait to see it all.

At sundown, Jean-Luc and I take the funicular to the butte and cherish the view of Paris, this time illuminated by the lights of the city. And then I get my wish. I see the light posts lit on Rue Foyatier, as we take our time down the steps. When we reach the bottom, we catch a cab to Saint-Germain-des-Prés for dinner.

As we sit outside Les Deux Magots, on this clear, crisp night in February with our chairs pushed together and Jean-Luc's arm around me, I can't help but notice how much I have changed. I smile wider and laugh harder. I am alert and aware, and I'm noticing every-thing—even the tiniest of details about Jean-Luc. Maybe it's because I don't want to miss a thing. Not a single thing about him. Not the way his lips curl when he smiles, or the way his eyebrows meet when he's worried, or the way his eyelids wrinkle when he's tired, or the way he sticks his feet outside the sheets when he sleeps. For the first time in a long time, I am actually living. I am here. I am alive. The changes that are happening to me—to us, have somehow revived everything that was dead in-side of me. Every day that we've spent together has left me in a state of complete euphoria.

Jean-Luc is like a drug I can't get enough of. And I want more of him. I crave for more.

I am addicted.

29

Books and Things

I wake up next to Jean-Luc.

His room is dim and warm. He's lying on his stomach, his slender body exposed. I tiptoe to the window to gaze out at the rooftops and manage to catch the beautiful sunrise, witnessing the break of a new day. My new day with Jean-Luc.

Is it luck or fate that I'm with him?

I sneak back into bed and kiss his shoulder and feel him move.

"What time is it?" he says, lifting his head ever so gently.

"It's early," I whisper.

He turns on his back with a tired smile.

I sit up and survey his room. An old dresser leans on the corner wall next to his window, the top drawers jutting out with sheets of paper filled with handwritten words.

"Do you keep everything you've ever written inside those drawers?"

"No, I'm sure I have a few scattered around the house," he says, sitting up.

"I'm still amazed at how you handwrite everything," I say, wondering if I'll ever get to read any of his work.

"It's what I'm used to," he says.

"And I'm used to my computer. It's the only way I can get my thoughts down fast enough."

"I don't own a computer."

"You don't own a computer?" I say, sitting up.

"No," he chuckles.

"Why not?"

"I don't need one."

"I don't know how you do it. I'm lost without mine."

"Where is your computer now?"

I sigh. "I forgot it in New York."

"Do you feel lost?"

I pause for a second.

"No. I guess not." I inhale deeply. "In a way, I am kind of relieved that I'm without it. Same with my phone." I shrug. "It's sort of liberating."

"Maybe you don't need them as much as you think you do."

"Maybe."

I lean forward, my head hanging on the side of the bed. "Are all your books in French?" I say, scanning the titles on the floor.

"Some are," he says, kissing my side.

I reach for a random book written in French and roll to my side to face Jean-Luc. "Read me something," I say, handing it to him.

"Why?" he asks, continuing to kiss me.

"Because I want to hear you read in French."

And so, he does. He reads me a whole page, while I watch him with a smile, marveling at his perfect face. Soon his voice fades into the background, and I get distracted examining his room once again. Worn out books scattered on the floor, a candle in a jar resting on his dresser, and a vintage Underwood Standard Typewriter on top of an antique folding writing desk.

He closes the book and reaches for a cigarette and a lighter from his side table. He watches me studying his things.

"What do you see?" he asks, lighting his cigarette.

"I see things that amaze me," I say, turning around to face him. "How old are you?" I ask, watching the smoke fill the air.

He leans back, squints his eyes, and inhales.

"I want you to guess," he says, exhaling.

"Oh, no" I chuckle. "I don't want to offend you if I'm wrong." I'm guessing he's probably in his mid-thirties, at least I hope. I glance at him once more and now think I could be wrong.

He laughs. "You won't offend me. Go ahead. Guess."

I take a deep breath and almost blurt, thirty-four, but instead I say, "I can't do it."

"I'm twenty-nine," he says.

I gulp. *Twenty-nine?*

"But I feel much older," he says, and puts the cigarette back in his mouth and inhales slowly. "How old are you?" he asks, blowing the smoke and resting his cigarette in the ashtray on the side table.

I gulp again.

"Take a guess," I say, only because I couldn't get myself to reveal my age. But making him guess only makes me nervous. What if he thinks I am older than thirty-four?

He turns to his side and studies my face, stripped of my usual makeup and creams. I avoid his eyes and pull the sheets up toward me.

"We're the same age," he says.

"We're not," I laugh.

"We're not?" he asks, leaning his head on his hand.

"I'm thirty-four," I say, surprised at how quickly I blurt it out. "But I feel much younger," I finish.

He smiles at me. "Thirty-four," he repeats. "That's a beautiful number."

"It is?"

"Yes, it is." He smiles again. "I like that you're thirty-four."

I stop fiddling with the sheets. I don't want to ask any more questions. I am content with everything he said.

"You amaze me," I say, gazing into his eyes.

"I do? Why?" he asks, moving in closer.

"I don't know why. You just do," I say, with a shrug.

But I do know why. He's different in many ways and more mature than any of the men I have dated in the past. He's an old soul, a beautiful soul. He's interesting and exciting and intense. And he makes me laugh. He's a simple man, and I love that most about him.

"Have you read them all?" I say, now lying on my stomach, facing the books on the floor.

"I have." He lies on his stomach to join me.

I rummage through his collection and pick up a few paperbacks, some in English and some in French and set them on the bed. I take one and roll on my back, reading it out loud in English, while Jean-Luc reads another book out loud in French. Then we switch books and he reads his in English and I try to read mine in French. I sound so horrible that we both laugh. Then our stomachs growl at the same time, and we laugh even harder.

"Breakfast?" he asks.

"Yes, please."

"What are you writing?" I ask, setting my cup of coffee on the table, watching Jean-Luc scribble away in his notebook.

"I can't tell you," he says, glancing at me.

"Will I get to read this one?"

"Maybe," he says, with a smile.

"OK," I say, leaning back on the wicker chair.

When my eyes settle on the street outside, I wonder. What if by some magical fluke, all this that's happening right now becomes my new life? That every morning, Jean-Luc and I will come to this café on Montparnasse and Rue Vavin, and we'll sit at this very table, this one, right by the door, and we'll each order our usual *café crème.* And Jean-Luc will write in his Moleskine notebook, and I'll people watch, and our life will be as simple as that. And it would be enough.

As I relish in this thought, a family of four walks in front of the café, dragging their suitcases down the sidewalk. When the little wheels rumble against the pavement, my body tenses up.

Today is Thursday. In a few days, I will be going home. And Jean-Luc has no idea.

30

See You Soon

At early dawn, I lie awake missing Jean-Luc.

Yet, he's right next to me. The thought that I haven't told him I'm leaving ails me. I know I should've said something at lunch or at dinner yesterday, especially when he had mentioned plans of us taking a trip next week to Versailles. But somehow, I couldn't get myself to tell him the truth. Instead, I said yes to all of our plans.

Now I can't sleep, because I know I have to tell him today, but I don't know how or when. I'm tossing and turning, trying to shake off these thoughts that I'm not ready to face. I don't want to wake him, so I roll out of bed and tiptoe to the kitchen. I grab a glass of water and stare out at the red sky.

I love being here.

And I don't want to change a thing.

But how can I live in this dream and still live my life in New York? How do I tell Jean-Luc that I don't want to leave, but I have to?

I take a few sips and leave my glass in the sink and tiptoe back to the room. I crawl into bed next to Jean-Luc who is now sleeping on his side, facing the wall. I lie on my back, staring at the dark ceiling until my eyes fold, seconds before the sunrise.

By the time I get up, Jean-Luc is already making coffee. I push the sheets off to the side and head to the kitchen.

"Good morning," I greet, noticing he's all dressed up in a light blue button-down and black dress pants. His thick hair slicked back, his face cleanly shaven.

"Good morning," he says, pouring our coffee into two white mugs.

I skip over and gingerly lift my mug from the table.

"Did you sleep well?" he asks.

"Very well. And you?"

"I did," he says, managing a quick smile.

"What should we do today?" I ask, sitting on the couch, tucking my legs in.

Jean-Luc checks his watch, looks at me, and then checks his watch again.

"Is everything OK?" I ask, sitting up.

"I'm sorry, but I have to be somewhere soon." He checks his watch a third time. "But I can see you tonight," he says.

"Oh," I reply, disappointed, but I quickly mask it with a smile. "Sure. Tonight, sounds great."

"Great," he says, searching for his keys.

Where is he going?

"You can stay here if you'd like. I can leave you my keys," he suggests.

"Thanks, but I should go back to the hotel. I forgot my phone there, and I need to make some calls anyway."

Everything I said is true. I do want to call Danielle and Cindy and tell them about my weekend. And I should probably check in with Craig regarding my last article.

Jean-Luc quickly sips his coffee.

"I want to drop you off. Let's share a cab," he says.

I agree and rush off to change.

It's a short ride to my hotel. I wish it were longer. Jean-Luc and I sit close to each other with my head resting on his shoulder, and my arm around his.

When the cab parks in front of my hotel, Jean-Luc says something in French to the driver, and he gets out and walks me to the glass doors of the hotel.

"I'll see you tonight," he says.

"I can't wait."

"I'll meet you here at eight," he says.

"At eight. Right here," I repeat, pointing at the spot we're standing on.

"Right here," he says, with a smile.

We kiss for a long second, and when he walks away, I wish I could pull him back and hold him a little while longer. When they drive off in a hurry, my heart slowly rips apart.

And I don't know why.

31

The Magazine

I unplug my phone when I get to my hotel room.

The screen says I have five messages, but instead of listening to my voicemails, I ring Danielle and she conferences Cindy straight away.

"How's Paris?" Danielle asks.

"I heard about the mystery guy. You're still coming to my wedding, right?" Cindy says, before I can even answer Danielle.

Ah, yes. Cindy's wedding, which until this moment, I forgot about how it falls on Valentine's Day. My *favorite* holiday. Luckily, I'm not a bridesmaid. As a matter of fact, no one is. She only wants to have her mother by her side. Perfect for Danielle since she's pregnant, and perfect for me because I'm not going. Of course, I'm kidding. I'm going. She's one of my closest friends. But I have to admit, a part of me does wish I could stay in Paris a while longer.

"Don't worry, I'm still flying back," I say at last, as the thought of leaving Jean-Luc saddens me.

"Good," Cindy says.

"Tell us what happened," Danielle says. I could tell from her voice that she is smiling.

"Well…" I say, pausing for a second.

"Tell us!" Cindy pleads.

"I spent the night at his place," I say, collapsing on the bed, staring dreamily at the ceiling.

"Seriously?" Danielle says.

"He must be something," Cindy says.

"Actually, I've spent more than one night with him," I say, smiling widely.

"Yup, he's definitely something," Cindy says.

"Lana, have you lost your mind?" Danielle says.

Yes, I have. And I'm fine with it.

"That may be a possibility," I say, with a laugh.

"Wait, who are we talking about? Is this the same guy you kissed on your first day, or is this the guy you were matched with at the café?" Cindy asks.

"Of course, it's the guy she got matched with at the café. She left the other one before, remember?" Danielle says. It's clear that she had filled Cindy in with all the details.

"I never got matched," I blurt.

"What!" they say, in chorus.

"What do you mean?" Cindy says.

"Lana, did you walk out again?" Danielle says.

"Well, a lot happened that day," I pause to take a deep breath. "I went back the following day to the café, as I had planned, but when I got there, it was closed."

"Closed?" Danielle asks.

"What do you mean? Do you mean closed for the day or closed for good?" Cindy asks.

"Closed for good," I explain.

"What the hell?" Cindy says.

I sit up. "You're not going to believe this, and I swear I'm not making this up." I pause. "The matchmaker passed away early that morning." My chest hurts, and the only memory I have of *Monsieur Dubois* flashes through my mind.

"What? He died?" Cindy says.

"Oh, my god!" Danielle says, closing the refrigerator door. "That's so sad."

"That is sad, and unbelievable," Cindy says.

"I couldn't believe it either. I felt horrible when I found out. I still feel horrible. Just thinking and talking about it now makes me want to cry."

"Please don't talk about crying, because it's going to make me cry. Don't you know I cry easily now?" Danielle says.

"I'm sorry. I don't want you to cry," I say, feeling my eyes water.

"Too late. I'm already crying," Danielle complains.

"OK, hold on. I don't get it. Who is this guy you spent the night with then?" Cindy says, confused.

"After I left the café, something happened. Something unexpected," I say.

"What happened?" they ask in chorus.

"After I heard about the matchmaker, I left the café and took a long walk to clear my head. And that's when it happened."

"What happened?" they ask again in chorus.

"I saw the Parisian boy again," I say, my heart melting as I tell the story.

"Are you serious?" Danielle says then blows her nose.

"Maybe he's stalking you," Cindy says.

"Yes, I'm serious, and no, he wasn't stalking me," I say, shaking my head.

"How did it happen?" Cindy asks.

"Tell us everything," Danielle says.

"Well, I had been walking for a while, and I couldn't stop crying. I literally had no control over my emotions. I was a complete wreck. I was in the midst of searching inside my purse for some tissue when I bumped into someone. I rushed off to a corner and heard someone say, *American.* I knew right away that it was him," I say.

"American?" they repeat, in chorus.

"Yes, that's what he calls me. But imagine him saying it in a French accent."

"OK," Danielle says, dreamily. "Yes, much better."

"All right, this is all too dramatic and too romantic, I'm about to puke," Cindy says, jokingly.

"Puke away, my friend," I say, chuckling.

"Where is he now?" Cindy asks.

"Does he have a name?" Danielle asks.

"Jean-Luc," I reply, falling back on the bed.

"Jean-Luc," they repeat.

"Definitely French," Danielle says.

"Why aren't you with him now?" Cindy repeats.

"He's running an errand or something. Anyway, we're seeing each other tonight," I reply.

"An errand?" Cindy asks.

"Who cares about the errand? Is he amazing in bed?" Danielle asks.

I shut my eyes and remember Jean-Luc's scent, his hair, his face, his lips, and his touch. I want time to fly faster, so I could fall into his arms again.

"He is amazing," I say, opening my eyes.

"A-ha! So, you do admit that you've slept with him!" Danielle says.

"Of course, she has. What do you think happened when they spent the night together? They just cuddled?" Cindy says, laughing.

"Leave me alone. I'm pregnant," Danielle grunts.

"But it didn't happen on the first night," I say.

"No need to explain," Cindy says. "I slept with Ben on the first night, and now we're getting married," she says.

"That's true," Danielle says. "Well, tell us more. On second thought, don't. I haven't had sex in months. This is torture," she says, laughing to herself.

"Lana, you are not missing my wedding. I don't care if this guy is *Mr. Right* or *Mr. Right Now*, you have got to be there. I need you there. You know I need you there," Cindy says.

"Don't worry. I already told you I'd be there."

"You can bring Jean-Pierre or Jean-Claude or what-ever his name is," Cindy says.

"It's Jean-Luc, and I don't think I can bring him."
Or can I?

"Hey, don't forget about my baby shower. You know it comes before the wedding," Danielle reminds both of us.

I can't believe I forgot about her baby shower until now.

"Yes, I'll be there," I reply, dreading the thought of leaving Jean-Luc. I love my friends, but deep inside, I wish I could put everything on hold and shut the world out and be with Jean-Luc a while longer.

"Of course, I'll be there, too," Cindy says.

"OK, good. I'll see you guys at my baby shower. Call me when you get back to New York, Lana. I need to hang up now. I'm off to a doctor's appointment," Danielle says.

"Yeah, I need to go, too. I have to pick up my wedding shoes since I can't trust my damn coordinator," Cindy says.

"OK. I miss you, guys," I say.

"Yeah, whatever. You're having too much fun there to miss us," Cindy teases.

"I miss you, too," Danielle says.

After our goodbyes, I doze off.

I wake up a couple of hours later with my phone buzzing on my stomach. I grab it, enter my password, and click on the first message.

"It's Craig. I got your email. The magazine is going to press tomorrow. I'll let you know how it goes."

I shut my eyes and listen to the second message.

"Lana, what's going on? It's been days, and I haven't heard from you. It's Craig. The article you wrote is getting a lot of buzz. Good buzz. Call me."

I open my eyes.

It's getting a lot of buzz? Good buzz?

I roll to my side and listen to the third message.

"Lana, it's Craig. They're going nuts, and they want more. We're receiving a ton of emails from our readers. They want more of you. Call me!"

My eyes widen. I sit up, ecstatic about the news. They liked my article? But I thought it was supposed to be my last. I can't believe they liked it. I can't stop smiling. I guess I didn't lose my job.

This is amazing.

I get to keep my job, and I found Jean-Luc.

Maybe writing for *Trend Magazine* isn't bad luck after all.

32

Perfection

As if I wasn't happy enough being with Jean-Luc and being in Paris, Craig's messages put me in an even better mood. I am still shocked about the success of my last article.

I call Craig right away.

He picks up after the first ring.

"Lana?" he answers. He has never sounded so eager to hear from me before.

"Hi, Craig. I got your messages," I say, smiling.

"Is it true? Are you in Paris?"

"Yes, I am," I say, smiling even wider now.

"Lana, your latest article is doing great. We're getting hundreds of emails from our readers asking about you, the café, the matchmaker, and Paris. They want to hear about what happened. Does the café exist? Is there a matchmaker? If so, what does he look like? They have a lot of questions. They want to know more. They want to know everything," he says.

"There's so much to tell. I wouldn't know where to start," I say, overwhelmed by the news. I'm not even sure I want to write about it. How do I tell my hopeful readers that I found the café, and that I was lucky enough to see the matchmaker? But now, he's gone. And the café is closed.

How would I explain all of that to them?

"Start somewhere. You don't have to tell them everything. But you have to tell them something. They want more, Lana. This is a good thing. It's good for business. It's good for you. For us," he says, enthusiastically.

"Does this mean I still have my job?"

"What do you mean? You always had your job," he says, laughing. "So, listen, here's what we're thinking. The last article you wrote could be your last one for 'Single and Loving It.'"

"I'm confused," I say.

"Well, we talked about it over here, and we think you're right. The readers are ready to hear about love and relationships. So, we're proposing a spin-off. A column that will give readers what they want—a column that will make them fall in love again."

"That sounds exciting," I say, my head spinning, thinking about all the new material I could write.

"You don't have to give me an answer right now. Give it some thought. But the sooner you get back to me, the sooner we can get started."

I cover the receiver with my hand and let out a silent scream. I love the idea of the new column.

"Yes, I'll do it," I say, not wasting any more time. "I'll write the spin-off. I'm ready."

"Great! I can't wait to share the good news with everyone here," he says. "By the way, when are you flying back to New York?"

"In a few days."

"OK, I'll call you. Let's chat at the office when you get back," he says.

"Sounds good. Thanks, Craig."

"Sure." He pauses. "So, how is Paris anyway?"

"Just perfect," I say, smiling widely.

"I'm sure it is. Enjoy it, Lana," he says.

I can't wait to tell Jean-Luc the good news.

It's 7:45 p.m. Jean-Luc will be downstairs any minute now. I scurry around the room in my underwear, deciding on what to wear. I want to look amazing tonight.

I lay out my navy-blue dress and my stockings on the bed. Then I put on some makeup, get dressed, and slip my feet inside my black pumps. After I put on my wool coat, I grab my purse and head downstairs. It's a few minutes to eight. The concierge greets me as I pass the lobby. I greet her back with a smile and head briskly toward the glass doors and push them open.

The sidewalk is empty.

Jean-Luc isn't here yet.

I check the time on my phone. It's 7:59 p.m. I'm a minute early.

I position myself in the same exact spot Jean-Luc and I had agreed to meet. I straighten out my dress, while I watch the cars zip by in all directions. It is such a beautiful night. I can see a lighted boat slowly moving in the river. A few minutes pass, I check the time. It's now 8:10 p.m. I check the streets and sidewalks for Jean-Luc. But still no sign of him anywhere.

It's OK.

He's running a little late.

I can wait.

I will wait.

The wind picks up, and the cold air spreads throughout my body. In every corner, there are lovers holding each other. Where is mine?

It's been twenty minutes. Has he forgotten about our date?

As time continues to tick, my body tenses up, and I worry.

Is Jean-Luc OK? Did something happen to him?

Or did he simply change his mind?

After freezing out in the cold, I trudge back to the hotel and run up to my room.

Was I stood up?

Perfect bliss or perfect miss?

As I lean my head on my hotel room window, staring down at the street below, a million thoughts fill my head. I obsess about all the possible reasons why Jean-Luc could've changed his mind about tonight and about me. Did we move too fast?

I scuff my feet toward the bed. I already know what Danielle is going to say once I tell her Jean-Luc didn't show up. She's going to tell me to sign me up for online dating. And I already know what Cindy will say. She'll say it wasn't meant to be. But I want it to be meant to be.

How could Jean-Luc not show up?

Wait. What if he did?

What if he is there right now?

I grab my purse and run down to the lobby, holding on to the thought that Jean-Luc could be outside looking for me. The concierge greets me again.

"*Bonsoir,*" she says, with a friendly nod.

"Bonsoir," I greet back. "I was wondering if anyone had asked for me recently?" I say, glancing at the glass doors.

"No one yet, *Madame,*" she says.

"OK, thanks," I say, looking out.

"Would you like me to call you when your guest arrives?" she asks, concerned.

I'm sure she can see the worried expression on my face, so I perk myself up and tell her I must have had the dates mixed up. Then I force a chuckle. I exit the glass doors and realize I don't have my coat on, and it's freezing, but I am too embarrassed to walk back in. So instead, I have coffee at the nearest café. Then I decide that maybe a walk would do me some good, and maybe the fresh air would clear my head. So, I purchase a sweatshirt and a scarf from a souvenir shop and roam the streets like I am on a mission to find something or get somewhere. But by the end of it all, when my feet hurt, I don't find anything or anyone, and I am exactly back to where I started.

The walk only reminds me of my solitude.

I guess that's it.

Another man, gone.

33

Antoine

An indescribable sense of torture lingers inside of me. I slept in spurts throughout the night, wondering what I could've said or done to drive Jean-Luc away, because it had to be my fault. It had to be me.

When I think of how hurt I was when Roy left me and how it took me three years to get over him, I am left speechless. Because how can a few days with a total stranger mean much more to me than the whole year I had with someone I knew? Or thought I knew. Is it possible to be more in love with someone that I had just met, than with someone that I was with longer? What defines it? What makes it real? What makes it possible? Or is it even possible?

By mid-morning, I step out. Hiding in my hotel room overanalyzing everything is only making me crazy. The minute I exit the hotel doors, I get the urge to go to Jean-Luc's apartment. But despite the few times I had been there, I have no idea where he lives, so, I don't hail a cab.

Instead, I walk for miles until the streets begin to look familiar. Then I doubt my decision. If Jean-Luc wanted to see me, he would have come over. He knows where to find me. But maybe that's just it. He doesn't want to see me.

I should turn around, yet I can't get myself to do it. I am desperate to find Jean-Luc's apartment. But as I go on, I realize the streets I thought that looked familiar look like everything else. I have wasted my time searching for a place I was never going to find. Maybe it's better this way because if I did see Jean-Luc, I don't know what I would say to him. But maybe I wouldn't need to say anything, because he would do all the talking. Besides, I am the one who needs an explanation, not him.

After failing to find Jean-Luc's apartment, I take a cab to his favorite café on Montparnasse and Rue Vavin. And while I wait for someone who may never show up, I try to distract myself. I search for the regulars—the characters that Jean-Luc had pointed out to me, but the only one here is the writer with the square face sitting at his usual table in the back.

Soon, I get engrossed with people watching. I observe the way they move and talk. I grow curious of what they are eating, what they are drinking, and even what books they are reading. Then at one point, I find myself staring at each little black and white tile on the floor. When I am done with that, I take a cab to Luxembourg Gardens and sit on a green metal chair and gaze out at the trees and the flowers. By late afternoon, I find myself climbing up the stairs on Rue Foyatier. Out of breath, I turn around, eager to face the stunning view. But there is no view. All I see is a thick fog covering all of Paris.

My luck has run out.

I hurry down the famous steps and hail a cab, with every intention of going back to my hotel. But when we drive past the café on Montparnasse and Rue Vavin, I ask the driver to stop. For some reason, I have the urge to go back. I am deflated, fighting the anguish inside of me by returning to the café, because somehow, doing so feels comforting. I sit at the same table, the one right by the door. I order a *café crème*, but only take one sip. I'm sitting here, waiting here, dawdling here, feeling worse than when I came in an hour ago.

I pay my bill and move toward the door. Now I am standing outside the doorway trying to figure out which direction to follow. I could easily take a cab back to the hotel, but I want to walk. So, I take a few steps to the right, and then I turn around and decide to go left. As I do, I hear someone say, "Excuse me. Are you lost?"

Before I could spin around to see who it is, a young man appears in front of me. He is a few inches taller than I am, he has dark brown hair with a boyish cut. His eyes are round and brown.

"I'm fine," I say, and continue past him.

"Are you sure you're not lost?" he asks again.

"I'm fine." I say and pick up my feet.

"You don't remember me?"

I pause and turn around.

"I was your waiter at the café," he says.

"You were?" I say, confused. Was I that oblivious that I didn't even notice him? I look harder, studying his face. "Oh, right," I say, shaking my head. "I'm sorry. I didn't recognize you. You look different."

"Different?" he says, approaching me.

"Yes, different. Were you wearing something else earlier?"

"My apron?" he says, lifting the rolled-up fabric in his hand.

"That must've been it," I say, with a dry laugh.

"Are you going home?" he asks.

"Home is far away," I say. "I'm heading back to my hotel."

"I walk you there," he says, in his heavy French accent.

"That's very kind of you, but I am going to take a cab."

He asks for the name of the hotel, ignoring what I had just said. So, I tell him.

He smiles and says, "Let's go."

"It's fine. I can take a cab."

But I don't want to take a cab.

"It's a beautiful night in Paris," he says, and beckons me. "We walk," he says, ambling past the now empty tables and chairs lined up on the sidewalk.

"I know you were my waiter earlier, but this is a little strange. I don't know you."

"*Ah, oui.* You are right." He approaches me with a smile. "I apologize. I'm Antoine," he says, extending his hand out. "And you are?"

"I'm Lana," I say, shaking his warm hand.

"You see? We are friends now. Let's go," he says, as if this is all it takes.

"Are you sure you know where to go?"

"Don't worry. I live in the area."

"Oh, OK."

"Let's go."

"All right." I say, surrendering.

What else am I going to do anyway? Sulk alone? I guess I could use the company.

During our long stroll, Antoine doesn't ask me where I am from or what I do for a living or even how long I will be staying in Paris. Instead, he points out random things I would've missed. A wet newspaper on a park bench, an empty plate on a table outside a bistro, a purple balloon tied to a car door parked alone in a dark alley. He is quick on his feet, hopping up and down the sidewalks, full of energy, smiling and laughing a lot. He is like a little kid. A little big kid.

About an hour later, we arrive at my hotel. I thank Antoine for walking with me.

"What will you do now?" he asks, as we stand by the glass doors.

"It's late. I guess I'll go to sleep."

"*Non*, it's early. Cigarette?" he says, pulling out a pack from his back pocket.

"Thanks, but I don't smoke."

He shrugs then lights a stick.

"Where do you live?" I ask, while I fight the urge to run upstairs and cry about Jean-Luc.

"Rue Vavin," he says, cheerfully.

"But isn't that where we were earlier?" I ask, confused.

He nods with a sneaky smile.

"Why did you walk me all the way here?"

He shrugs. "Because you looked lost, and I am in no hurry to go home," he says.

"That's very kind of you. Thank you."

"You're welcome," he says, and takes another drag and blows off the smoke then offers me his cigarette. I shake my head.

Antoine sits on the sidewalk, as I remain standing.

"That was a long walk," I say.

"Sit," he says, tapping the spot next to him as he takes another drag.

"What am I doing?" I say, under my breath, proceeding to sit down next to him.

"Where is your boyfriend?" he says.

I laugh, surprised by his question. "Where is my boyfriend?" I repeat. "That's a really good question." I shake my head. "Well, I don't have one."

"I don't believe it," he says, squinting his eyes at me.

"Believe it," I say, chuckling. I turn to face him.

"Where is your girlfriend?"

"I don't have a girlfriend."

"I don't believe it."

We chuckle.

"Love is complicated," he says.

"Love is complicated," I repeat.

We both sigh at the same time and share a laugh.

"You know what?" I say, folding my legs.

"What?"

"I will have a cigarette."

He smiles and hands me one, leaving his cigarette hanging in his mouth while he lights mine.

"Tomorrow is my birthday," Antoine says.

"Do you mean today? It's past midnight."

He checks his watch. "Ah, *oui*. Today."

I ask him how old he is. He says he just turned twenty-five. He is only a few years younger than Jean-Luc, but he seems much younger. Or maybe Jean-Luc seems much older.

We finish our cigarettes and keep each other company for a while longer until I decide it's time to go. When Antoine leaves, I cross the street and walk to Pont Neuf. I look down and notice a group of kids, probably in their early twenties, sitting by the river, smoking, drinking, and laughing. I press my elbows against the stone bridge and focus my eyes on the dark, silky water. As I let the cold air embrace me, I wonder where Jean-Luc could be.

34

Farewell, Paris

A couple of days ago, I was worrying about how to tell Jean-Luc that I would be leaving soon. It turns out, I didn't have to worry, because he would be the one leaving me.

At a little past eight in the morning, I reluctantly call the front desk, and in a desperate, but polite tone, ask if I have any messages. Josephine politely tells me that I do not. An hour later, I call again and again and again. Josephine finally suggests that she could call my room if I had any messages.

I've been sitting here listless in bed with no intentions of moving. I'm slowly accepting the fact that Jean-Luc stood me up and isn't coming back.

Oh, Paris. How did you make me fall in love and manage to break my heart, all in a matter of days?

I guess this confirms that when it comes to love, my bad luck isn't over after all. Because the moment I accepted to write my new column, Jean-Luc never came back. But is it the magazine's fault, or are these mere co-incidences?

I should've left last night.

Why am I still here?

Is it because a part of me wants to believe that Jean-Luc would suddenly show up and the concierge would call me, and I would run downstairs and everything would be fine. Jean-Luc would cover me with kisses, and when he begins to apologize, I would forgive him before he could even finish.

I want to believe that all of this could happen. But I know none of it will, or else it would have happened already. Maybe what we had, happened too fast and it had to end as quickly as it began.

Languid, I lay my head on my flat hotel pillow with my eyes shut, pouring out tears, driving myself crazy with my thoughts.

This can't be good.

I need to pull myself together.

I sit up, brush my cheeks with my hands, and reach for my phone. I dial Cindy's number. I need to talk to someone.

"Hello?" Cindy answers.

"He never showed," I say, holding back my tears.

"Lana? What happened? Are you OK?" she asks, concerned.

"I waited that night, but he never showed. What am I doing wrong? Why do they all leave me?" I ask, my lips quivering.

"Oh, no. Believe me, Lana, it has nothing to do with you. They're just not the right ones. That's all it is. You're perfect the way you are, and they can't handle it," she replies, trying to ease my pain.

"Thanks, but I know I am not perfect. Not even close. Maybe that's why Jean-Luc changed his mind," I say.

"Honey, I'm sorry. I don't know what to say."

"I'm so tired of it all. I'm tired of being alone. I thought everything was changing for me. I was starting to believe I had found the right guy for me. He made me feel needed and wanted, and with him, I was the happiest I have ever been. He was the one who was perfect—not me. Too perfect for me. Maybe that was the problem," I say, with a break in my voice.

Cindy sighs. "I hate to say this, Lana, but maybe it was meant to be a whirlwind romance. You said you wanted to go there to find romance, right? Well, you found it, and unfortunately, that's all it was." She takes a deep breath. "Come home, Lana. What are you still doing there? Being there will only make you more miserable."

I know she's right. What am I still doing here? What am I still hoping for? A fairy tale? It's not going to happen.

"Yeah, I know," I say, under my breath.

"Come home now. I'll take you out for some drinks when you get back," she says, trying to perk me up.

"It hurts," I mutter.

"Oh, Lana. Don't worry, you'll find someone else soon. I really believe that. But you have to believe that, too."

"Yeah." That's all I could say.

"Call me when you get back," she says.

"I will."

After we hang up, I dump my clothes back into my suitcase. I shower and change into a pair of jeans and a sweater. I pull my hair back into a bun and look around the room one last time. And all I see is Jean-Luc. I can't shake him off even if I want to. Even if I need to. Maybe the lady on the train was right. Parisian men are horrible. Why didn't I listen to her? I could've saved myself from all this misery. But maybe it's not about Parisian men. Maybe when it comes to love, she and I are simply the unlucky ones.

I drag my suitcase down the dreadful staircase. Somehow everything feels heavier compared to when I first arrived. With each step I take, down to the lobby, my heart aches more.

"Any messages?" I ask, one last time.

Josephine tightens her lips and shakes her head.

"I'm sorry, but I need to check out a day early," I say, aware I had originally booked the room until tomorrow.

"Oui, Madame. No problem." She starts typing. "We hope you enjoyed your stay," she says.

I nod with a blank stare.

When she hands me my receipt, I thank her and hurry out the glass doors and never look back.

35

Plane Insane

I charged another plane ticket to my credit card.

This time I overspent on a first-class seat for a direct flight home. It was the only one available in the next hour, and I didn't want to wait any longer.

I am sitting by the window, next to an empty seat, which is perfect. I need to be alone. No woman next to me springing off her seat. No sad love stories that I don't need to hear. I have my own.

Hours later, the plane touches down on LaGuardia Airport. I want to scream, as though someone had pulled the Band-Aid off my wounded heart when the cut had not yet healed. This one is going to scar.

The cab ride home is a quick reintroduction to the real world, with the stench inside and the sticky seat and the chaos outside. I watch the cab driver change lanes like a madman, as he tries to get me to my destination in a hurry, even though I am in no rush to go back home. But he doesn't know that. It is clear that I am no longer in Paris and no longer with Jean-Luc. The balmy weather and the placid streets are all in my past. I am back to my old life, my old reality. And whether I like it or not, it's all I've got now.

I plan to call Cindy and Danielle, but only after I have allowed myself to cry one more time. Tears are the only friends I need at the moment, and well, I have quite a lot of them.

I arrive at my apartment at a little past nine in the evening, dragging my suitcase inside my bedroom and collapsing on the bed. I am relieved to be back, but at the same time, I wish I wasn't home. The familiarity of my sheets comforts me, but the memories of Paris haunt me.

I guess it's time I give up on follies and accept the perils of love and relationships—the ugly side of it all. How can bliss only be present in the beginnings? Is it because we know nothing about the other person, and we are blinded by the unblemished surface that does nothing but fool us? And when the surface slowly breaks and the truth creeps out, bliss falls through the cracks and ruins everything. Is this what love is supposed to be like? And if so, why do we keeping wanting to fall in love? Why do we even bother?

As reality slowly seeps in, I realize how foolish I was for fleeing to Paris—all because of an article I had read in a magazine. I sit up and toss my purse on the bed. Some of the contents fall out. I glare at the mess that now crowds my bed. Red lipstick, powder, coins, and the napkin I wrote on, lay on top of a folded sheet of paper. I take the paper and unfold it. It is the illustration of a sad face of a woman. My sad face, revealing how I felt then, and how I am feeling now. I roll to my side and curl up into a ball.

A few hours later, I wake up from my phone ringing. It's Cindy.

"Hey," I greet, with no emotion.

"Glad you're back. You sound awful."

"Thanks."

"Are you tired?" she asks.

"Nope." But I am.

"Need a drink?"

"Yup." A lot.

"Great. Get dressed. I'm taking you out. I'll pick you up in twenty minutes," she instructs.

"OK," I reply, still void of emotion.

Forget resting. I might as well stay up drinking.

36

Hangover

Getting inebriated when you're jet-lagged is a terrible idea. I've thrown up at least four times, and I'm pretty sure I'm not done. It's six in the morning. I haven't slept much. Cindy dropped me off at home around 2:00 a.m. I've spent the last hour sitting next to my toilet. I'm supposed to meet Cindy this afternoon to accompany her to some wedding errands. I'm not fit to go, but I have to go, because I promised her I'd help. It's the least I can do. Especially since she bought me all those drinks last night and listened to me whine and groan about my sorry love story.

My head is throbbing. I already took aspirin half an hour ago. I'm still waiting for it to work.

I pluck myself off the floor and splash cold water on my face. I gargle and drag myself back to bed. It feels worse when I'm lying down. Everything is spinning. I shut my eyes and pray the spinning stops. I need to sleep.

Hours later, the doorbell wakes me.

My headache is gone.

The doorbell rings again.

It must be Cindy.

I open my eyes and force myself up. It's one in the afternoon. I drag my feet to the door and press the inter-com button.

"Who is it?" I ask.

"It's Cindy. Let me up," she says.

I buzz her in and unlock the front door.

I walk to the bathroom to freshen up.

I swear I'm never drinking again.

"Lana?" Cindy calls out, as I hear my front door shut.

"In the bathroom!" I yell.

"Are you only getting ready now?" she says, approaching my room.

She walks toward the bathroom and sees me with my hair and clothes in complete disarray.

"Oh, honey. You look terrible."

"Thanks," I reply facetiously.

"Why don't you get ready?" she suggests.

"I was about to shower," I playfully push her toward the living room. "Wait out there. I'll be ready soon."

"Do you have any coffee?" she asks, exiting my bed-room.

"No, but I would love some."

"We'll get some on our way to the appointment."

"OK," I say, shutting the bathroom door and turning on the shower.

During our cab ride to the flower shop, Cindy states the obvious and tells me that I had a bit too much to drink last night. Apparently, at one point, I confessed my story to a group of men, sitting at a table by the restrooms. I guess I had planned on freshening up but ended up talking to them for a while and chugging down a few more drinks. Cindy eventually had to pull me away, drag me to the restroom, then took me home.

"They probably thought I was so pathetic," I say, shaking my head. "Were they really listening to me? Did anyone say anything?" I ask, afraid of her reply.

Cindy tells me that some guy who was twice my size put his arm around me and said, "He must have had a good reason for standing you up, pretty little lady." And after that, Cindy yanked me away, and off we went.

Maybe he was right. Maybe Jean-Luc *did* have a good reason. But what is it?

The flower shop has a small kitchenette across from the waiting area. I help myself to a cup of black coffee, which I plan on refilling soon. The powerful fragrance permeating in the air is not helping my current state. My eyes dart around searching for a restroom in case I have to throw up. But as I scan the room, I notice Cindy struggling with her centerpiece arrangement, which frankly, looks fine to me. A vase with a bunch of flowers bunched up together inside—what else is there to it?

"Are you sure you like it?" she asks me for the tenth time, with her arms crossed, tilting her head left and right, staring at the same arrangement we've been looking at for half an hour.

"It's fine," I reply, gaping at the tall vase filled with white flowers.

"Just fine?" she asks, checking every angle.

I look again and pretend to contemplate it for a while.

"I love it," I say, and well, it's true. I do love it. But then again, all the arrangements look good to me.

"I love it, too." She bops her head in agreement. "It's exquisite. Simply exquisite," she says smiling, her arms now resting on her sides.

A couple of hours later, we stop for pizza, then head over to meet with the DJ. A band is not even an option for the couple-to-be. They prefer a DJ to play their favorite tunes.

"The music has to be perfect. I need to make sure I give him a list of every song I want to hear and how and when I want it played," she explains to me.

Cindy clearly knows what she wants. I had no idea she could be this particular. But then again, what do I know about weddings? When Danielle tied the knot, it was an intimate affair that they planned in three months. Her sister helped her plan the whole thing. The only time Cindy and I showed up to help her was when she picked out her wedding gown.

"This is the place," she says, checking the address on a sheet of paper. I follow her into a store somewhere in West 81st street.

"This is a record store. I thought you were meeting with a DJ?"

"We are. He owns this place," she says, entering ahead of me.

The place is small and grungy. There are wooden boxes full of old records in the middle of the room and some across the walls. There is barely any room to move around.

"Are you sure you want this guy to play your music?" I whisper to Cindy, after we notice "Heart of Glass" is playing by Blondie. We laugh.

A minute later, a tall skinny guy with round spectacles appears from the back and walks toward us. His hair is dark and greasy, and he's wearing a plaid shirt and ripped jeans.

"Cindy?" he says.

"Yes, that's me. Tim?" she asks.

"That's me. Nice to meet you," he says, shaking Cindy's hand and glances at me.

"This is my friend, Lana. Lana, this is Tim."

Tim and I shake hands.

"I've heard a lot of great things about you. I can't wait to show you my music list," Cindy says.

"Oh, thanks. I have a few forms for you to fill out. Why don't you come on back?" he says and leads the way.

"If it's OK, I'll scan through the records," I say.

"Suit yourself. We'll be here if you need us," Tim says. Cindy smiles at me then turns around and follows him to the back.

I walk through the aisles, in between wooden boxes, running my fingers through the stacks of records. I look through a box from the 70s. Nothing appears to be in order. Rolling Stones, Marvin Gaye, Bee Gees, AC/DC, Donna Summer. It makes me wonder what Cindy's list looks like.

The store remains empty. I'm the only customer, and I'm not even a customer. I simply tagged along. I've been here now for at least twenty minutes, and I haven't seen anyone else enter.

I survey the walls and the boxes against the wall. This place is amazing. It has everything. As I approach the back of the room, a familiar song plays. It takes me a second to realize what it is, and when I do, my knees weaken. It's the same song Jean-Luc played in his apartment the first time I was there. My eyes water, a clear vision of his face stuck in my head.

"Wish you were here," I mumble to myself, my throat drying up. I look up and notice Cindy and Tim making their way toward me, talking and laughing.

My tears are about to pour.

"We're back," Cindy announces.

When they get closer, I swerve around.

"Sorry, I need to step out. I got something in my eye," I say, sprinting for the door and slapping on my sunglasses.

37

Craig

Cindy and I part ways on Fifth Avenue between West 33rd and 34th Streets, where she's meeting her fiancé.

Meanwhile, I can't wait to go home and catch up with sleep. But in the midst of trying to hail a cab, Craig calls and asks me to stop by the office as soon as possible. I say yes, regardless of my current disposition.

Despite how happy as I was hearing about the surprising success of my last article, I am dreading this meeting. I mean, what do I have to offer now? There is nothing to tell. There probably won't be any for a long time. Unless I lie again, but what's the point? How do I fake bliss and pretend I was in a fairy tale when neither one exists?

Minutes later, I enter *Trend Magazine* with my head down low. My hair is flat, and I have no makeup on. I hide behind my sunglasses, hoping no one notices me.

"How was Paris, Lana?" someone asks in a high-pitched tone. I don't know who, because my eyes are glued to the floor.

"Great. It was great," I reply, clenching my jaw.

I keep going. Craig's office is at the end of the floor. I speed up past a dozen cubicles.

"I loved your last article," someone else praises. I nod and smile and continue walking never lifting my head, despite more positive comments coming at me. I hurry the last few steps toward Craig's office.

Craig is sitting at his desk with his tie over his left shoulder, working on a chicken salad.

"Welcome back, Lana," he says, getting up to hug me. I hug him back. I don't remember Craig ever being this chipper.

"Thanks," I reply. "Do you mind if I close the door?"

"Not at all."

I push the door shut and walk over to a chair close to the window. But I don't sit down.

"Are you OK?" he asks, observing me.

"I'm fine," I say, avoiding his eyes.

"Are you sure?"

"Yeah, I'm fine. Just tired. I arrived yesterday," I say, skipping the other details.

Craig sits down, pushes his chicken salad to the side, raises his legs on the table, and studies me. I can sense his eyes peering through my thick, dark glasses.

"I'm excited about the new column," I blurt, with a quick smile. Craig's face lights up.

"The emails are still coming in, Lana. Everyone wants to know about your trip. They want to hear about Paris and the matchmaker. They want to know about what happened in Paris. You gained a ton of new readers with this article."

I cringed each time he mentioned *Paris*.

"Wow," I shake my head. "I can't believe it," I say, doing my best to sound enthusiastic.

But deep inside, the thought of disappointing more people with my fake articles sickens me. I should quit now and spare them the fictionalized stories I'm about to write.

"I have even bigger news," he says.

"Bigger news?" I say, falling on the seat behind me. Whatever it is, I don't think I can handle it right now.

He whips his legs off the desk.

"A major publisher has shown a lot of interest in your column. There have been talks of a possible book deal," he says, leaning forward.

"Book deal?" I ask, surprised.

I have always dreamt of writing a book and getting it published, but not even this right now is enough to mend me.

"Yes," he says, nodding his head rapidly. "They are interested in possibly a memoir about your trip to Paris. They want to hear about the café and the matchmaker and everything that happened along the way."

I cringed again when he said *Paris* and cringed even more when he said *matchmaker*.

I swallow hard. "Wow," is all I could manage to say.

"If you're interested, which I'm sure you are, we'll need to send them a proposal. Soon." He leans back and rests his feet back on the table. "What do you think?"

I get up and stand by the window. I've been dreaming of a book deal for years, and here it is now. But I don't know if I'm ready to write about Paris, or the matchmaker, or the café, or about Jean-Luc. I don't even know if I will ever be ready. But I can't tell Craig. At least not now.

"Lana?" Craig says, snapping me out of my thoughts.

"Sorry, I'm still in shock," I say, forcing a higher pitch in my tone. "It's wonderful news, but I'm a bit over-whelmed at the moment. Can I have some time to think it over?"

"Sure, of course you can. I know you're tired from your trip, but when you're all rested, let's talk more." He gets up and walks me to the door. "Great things are hap-pening here, Lana. Great things."

I smile and thank Craig.

"Go get some rest, and I'll call you in a couple of days."

I rush out of the building and take a cab home. I get to my apartment in record time. I kick off my shoes, turn off my phone, and climb into bed. I pull my blanket over my head and close my eyes.

A couple of hours later, I wake up with my sunglasses still on. I take them off and place them on the side table. It's 11:00 p.m. My stomach growls. I trudge to the kitchen and open the fridge. It's empty, except for a box of old Chinese food leaking sauce, some butter, and half a jar of mayonnaise.

I reach for my phone and order a medium pepperoni pizza. I doze off on my orange chair and wake up to the sound of the doorbell. A few slices later, I drag myself to the bedroom and roll back to bed.

38

Baby Shower

It's February 12.

Today is Danielle's baby shower, which means Cindy's wedding is in two days. *Two days.*

I love my friends dearly, but a part of me wishes I could skip the events and hide under the sheets and wallow in my own misery. But I know I have to go. And of course, I'm going.

I arrive at the baby shower a little past two in the afternoon. Danielle's sister, Diane, organized the party. She has four kids of her own and loves the chaos that comes with it. I've always believed that some women are born to be mothers. I personally don't think I'm one of them. Diane, on the other hand, was meant to be one. And she's a damn good one, too.

Danielle's house is beautifully decorated with blue everything. Blue balloons, blue ribbons, and blue signs everywhere. Perfect color to represent how I'm feeling. But seeing the color blue is refreshing in a way. At least it's not red everything because I've seen enough red hearts, red roses, and red greeting cards to last me a long time.

Diane does a spectacular job transforming Danielle's dining room into a fun restaurant setting. The group is intimate and low-keyed with mostly family and a few close friends. Cindy arrives shortly after me and appears calmer than I had expected.

"You look relaxed," I greet her.

"Trust me, I may look relaxed, but I've got a lot on my mind. There's still a lot to do." She pauses to study me.

"You doing OK?" she says.

"Yeah, I got some sleep."

"Good for you. Where's Danielle?" she asks.

"I don't know. I haven't seen her."

We both survey the room.

Minutes later, Danielle shows up in the living room, looking rested and happy to see everyone. Her belly has grown exponentially since the last time I saw her. It must be strange having a baby growing inside of you. The thought alone frightens me.

"How are you doing?" I ask, hugging her.

"I'm fine. The baby has been very active today. He must know about the party." We chuckle. "Anyway, how are you?" she asks.

"I'm good," I reply, wondering if Cindy had filled her in with my Paris trip. Either way, I wasn't going to bring it up. Today is all about her. Besides, I don't want to stress her out or bore her with my pathetic love life. Not now anyway.

After hours of chatting and participating in baby shower games, Danielle opens her presents. We watch her living room quickly transform into a nursery. It's amazing how much she has already accumulated, and the baby is not even born yet. As she goes through each gift, I find myself amused by the variety of products I have never seen before. I didn't know there was such a thing as a Boppy Pillow.

Hours later, Cindy, Diane, and I help clear the mess at Danielle's before we all head out.

Surprisingly, I enjoyed the party, probably because of all the delicious cupcakes I kept shoving down my throat. Being there was a good distraction from my life, at least for a moment. It also helped that no one asked about me or about my column or about Paris. I thought for sure that someone would, especially since we were all girls. But no questions were asked. Everyone spoke about babies, giving birth, and everything else I couldn't relate to. It felt good to be left alone and be focused on someone else's life for a change.

Danielle is going to be a mother. I still can't fathom how quickly everything has changed. Two years ago, we were bar-hopping and free. Now she's married and pregnant and Cindy's wedding day is two days away. I'm happy for them. I'm happy when they're happy, and from the looks of it, they both look very happy. I want to be happy. I want to look happy and be happy. Oh, happy, happy, happy. OK, enough of that.

As soon as I get home, I curl up in bed holding my pillow—the only companion I have these days. I find it hard to sleep. I can't stop thinking about my new column and the possible book deal and Cindy's upcoming nuptials. But most of all, I can't stop thinking about Jean-Luc. How could perfection only last for a few days? How could bliss only whisk me by? Why couldn't any of it stay?

How foolish of me to expect so much more from what Jean-Luc and I had. I thought we would be spending more time together—at least another night. I thought I would be calling Danielle and Cindy apologizing for how I would miss their special events, and not even feel a wee bit sorry, because I would be too busy and too happy to care. But I thought wrong. Everything seemed to be going great. I should have known that it would all be temporary.

I guess the one good thing from all of this is I'm finally over Roy. Of course, being with Jean-Luc had a lot to do with it. But now I'm left trying to find closure with Jean-Luc. Or am I again expecting something that may never come? Maybe coming back to New York is my closure.

But will it be enough?

39

A Little Black Dress

One more day before Cindy's wedding. I called her this morning to check on how she's doing. She and her fiancé were going through their wedding list and sounded a bit frazzled. I called Danielle to check on her, but she and her husband were going through their hospital list and sounded preoccupied.

So, I left my apartment, and now I'm at the café across the street, struggling to drink my espresso. Seeing it reminds me of Jean-Luc. I flag the waiter and ask him to take it away and replace it with a huge cup of latte. The waiter is steadfast. I only take a couple of sips.

After breakfast, I take a cab to SoHo. I need to find a dress to wear to the wedding. But even looking at dresses reminds me of Jean-Luc. I think about the dress I wore the night he didn't return, and for a moment, I get the urge to go home and burn it, as if doing so would help me heal and make me forget about Paris. But I fight the urge, and I persevere until I find a simple little black dress that perfectly covers my aching heart. Then I head home.

During my walk, I contemplate about my new column. If I can't find anything to write about, then why should I even bother? I should quit writing. I have no material. I lost it all. But I know I can't quit. I don't want to lose this new opportunity with *Trend Magazine.* If I lose this, too, I have nothing. Besides, the job suits me. It gives me the freedom to work from anywhere and live my life.

I stop by a grocery store before going home, and even here, I struggle. Seeing wine and cheese instantly reminds me of Paris and Jean-Luc. Instead of turning away, I buy two bottles of chardonnay, three types of cheeses, and a baguette. On my way to the register, I notice notebooks on display and end up buying one of those, too. Because even that reminds me of Jean-Luc.

Now I'm sitting at my dining table, slicing cheese, eating bread, and drinking wine. I start with a glass, and soon, help myself to the bottle, which I chug with every bite. I do all this while sobbing. I must be slowly losing my mind, chewing and crying all at the same time. But I want to do it. I need to do it. In a twisted way, it feels good. I miss Jean-Luc. Maybe part of why I wallow in my feelings and drink wine and eat cheese is to somehow pretend we are still together. Like I am still in Jean-Luc's apartment and nothing ever changed. I would love to go back to that time. But it is clear that there is no dim room with a stack of books scattered on the floor. There is no Jean-Luc. And I am not in Paris. I am in New York. Alone.

My suitcase remains on my bedroom floor, next to my closet. The same spot I left it when I arrived. For a moment, I think about unpacking, but I can't get myself to do it. So, I let my suitcase sit there like a permanent fixture waiting to get old and dusty, and then forgotten.

My phone rings. The sound snaps me out of my glum state.

"Hey, Cindy," I greet, clearing my throat. "How's it going?" I follow up, trying hard to sound cheery.

"Lana, I have a stupid question to ask you," she says.

"Ask away," I say.

"We're looking at the table settings and place cards and we have you sitting next to a plus one, because, well, you originally RSVP'd with a plus one. Should I cancel the plus one?"

Is she seriously asking me this question?

"What do you think?" I reply, perturbed by the question.

"Oh, Lana. I'm sorry. I knew it was a dumb question," she says, in an apologetic tone.

"It's OK. Don't worry about it. I will be going alone, unless the homeless guy next to the corner store wants to be my date," I say, forcing a laugh.

"Don't say that. I'm sorry I asked. I just wasn't sure, so I thought I'd ask you anyway," she says, embarrassed.

"It's OK. It was my fault for not telling you to change that," I say, quickly sipping the last few drops of wine from the bottle and then spinning it on the dining table. It points to me.

"So, hey," she pauses, "how are you doing anyway?" she says, sounding concerned.

"I'm OK. Busy unpacking," I lie, spinning the bottle again. It points back to me.

"That's good," she says.

"Well, I have to go unpack," I say, rushing her off the phone.

"Lana?"

"Yeah?"

"We are going to party tomorrow, OK? I am going to live on that dance floor all night long, and I'm taking you with me," she says, in an enthusiastic tone.

"Terrific," I reply, with no emotion.

"Oh, Lana. It's my wedding day. Can you please pretend to cheer up a bit? For me?" she pleads.

That's all I have been trying to do all day. Pretend to cheer up a bit. But she's right. Just because I'm miserable doesn't mean I have to drag everyone else down with me.

I inhale deeply. "I'll be fine tomorrow, Cindy. I promise."

"OK. I love you."

"Love you, too."

"I'll call you later," she says.

"Yup. Bye," I say, and hang up the phone.

I open the second bottle of chardonnay and return to my room.

Hours later, I wake up with a throbbing headache.

40

The Wedding

I must have dozed off again, because I just woke up.

It's noon.

I stretch my arms and take a deep breath.

It's here.

February 14 has arrived.

No stomachaches. Only heartaches.

I turn to my side and force myself out of bed. I grab the half bottle of wine and head to the kitchen. I open the fridge, chill the wine, and nibble on a slice of cheese. Then I shower and change into my little black dress and curl my hair.

Today is about Cindy.

I am not going to let it be about me.

I arrive at the church a few minutes before the ceremony commences. The church is packed with about 200 people all dressed in dark suits and cocktail dresses. I find a seat toward the front, next to Danielle and her husband, Ted.

"Isn't this exciting?" Danielle whispers to me.

"Yes, it is," I reply, embracing the fact that Cindy is about to get hitched.

The crowd grows silent as the organist hits the first keys to Bach's Air on the G String. Diane's kids are the flower girls and ring bearer. They look adorable in their little white outfits walking down the aisle. As they clear the aisle, the music stops and everyone rises. The doors open, and the music resumes. Cindy enters the church wearing her beautiful lace gown. She looks stunning. Her father walks her down the aisle with his chin up and his arm tightly wrapped around hers.

My eyes dart across the room toward the altar where I get a glimpse of the groom. He is gazing at Cindy with the most genuine expression of love. I understand now that every little stress Cindy went through to plan this day has paid off. She is marrying the man of her dreams, and I can see he loves her dearly.

Cindy and her father approach the altar. As my eyes water, I hear Danielle sobbing next to me.

"It's my hormones," she mutters, holding a small box of tissues. Ted rubs her back.

The moment Cindy's father releases her hand and leads her over to Ben, their new life together begins. Cindy and Ben lock eyes and hold hands, as giant smiles form on their faces. When the priest speaks, I fade off to Paris, imagining that I am reuniting with Jean-Luc. By the time I snap out of it, the couple is kissing and everyone, including myself, start cheering. Danielle, on the other hand, is still crying.

A hundred photo sessions later, we arrive at the Starlight Roof of the Waldorf Astoria for the wedding reception. Everything looks extravagantly exquisite. The flowers look amazing. Cindy definitely made all the right decisions. I spot Tim, the DJ, at the edge of the dance floor wearing a black suit. And as expected, Cindy's playlist is being played exclusively.

I am sitting with Danielle, Ted, and Cindy's immediate family. Cindy and Ben are sitting alone at their sweetheart table positioned in the middle of the room.

As dinner gets served, Cindy leaps on the dance floor and sways her hips and arms to every song playing. She is beaming from ear to ear, and the best part is, Ben joins her the entire time. He doesn't enjoy dancing, but tonight, he is going to dance—no matter what, because it makes his bride happy, and that makes him happy.

Soon, Cindy wastes no time and pulls me to the dance floor. I dance to a couple of songs before I park myself next to the open bar and chug down one drink after another. Then I propel back to the packed dance floor and join Cindy and Ben. Danielle and Ted manage to follow our lead with Danielle only swaying her arms up in the air.

By the end of the night, my hair is damp with sweat, and my feet are killing me. Danielle and Ted head out a little early. A couple of hours later, I bade goodbye to the newlywed couple and catch a cab home.

I fight to keep my eyes open the entire ride. Minutes later, I arrive at my building. I step out of the cab with my shoes off and tiptoe to the front door.

As I dig inside my purse for my keys, I hear someone's voice.

"Hi, Al."

41

Uninvited

I thought this was over.

Why is he here?

Didn't I close this door weeks ago?

I turn around reluctantly.

"R-Roy?" I utter, confused.

"Hi, Al." He smiles. "You look all dressed up."

"Cindy got married today." I shake my head. "Roy, it's almost midnight. What are you doing here?" I ask, sobering up quickly, baffled by his sudden appearance.

"I needed to see you," he blurts.

"W-what?" I reply, still shocked that he's standing in front me.

"I can't stop thinking of you." He hands me a bouquet of flowers, and I don't know whether to take them or not.

Why is he doing this now?

"What is this for? You're three years too late. Seriously, what were you thinking coming here tonight?" I ask, still fighting the alcohol lingering inside my body.

"I want to talk. That's all," he says.

"Fine. Call me in the morning," I say, pulling out the keys from my purse.

"Al, I miss you," he says, out loud.

Is this a joke?

I turn around to face him.

"What do you want me to do about it?"

"Please let me come up," he begs.

"For what?"

"To talk. Just talk."

"Go home, Roy. It's late," I say, turning around again.

"Please. I waited hours for you," he pleads.

"I didn't ask you to do that."

"I know you didn't." He takes a deep breath. "At least accept the flowers."

With hesitation, I move closer, and as I take the flowers, he gently grabs my hand.

"Please, Al. Give me a chance to say what I need to say."

His eyes are desperate. What do I do? Do I let him in? I thought I was done with all of this.

"You have thirty minutes," I demand.

"Thank you," he says, relieved.

He follows me to the door. While I turn the key, everything in my body tells me I am making a mistake.

But I do it anyway.

Roy follows me to the elevator. We don't say a word the entire ride. After we exit, I speed ahead of him and approach my door. I turn the key and let myself in first. He trails behind me.

As I proceed to the kitchen, Roy sits at the edge of my couch.

"Do you want something to drink?" I say.

"What do you have?" he asks.

I open the fridge and notice the half bottle of wine.

"Water and wine," I reply.

"Wine is fine."

I wanted him to say *water*.

"Wine it is," I say, pouring him a glass. "Do you think you can finish it in half an hour?" I say, jokingly. But I'm not kidding.

He forces a smile.

"It's 11:30. I'm keeping track," I say, sounding crude.

He glances at his watch and looks at his glass.

"Where is yours?" he asks.

"I've already had too much to drink."

We sit in silence for a long minute.

"I'm sorry I didn't show up that night," I say, even though I didn't mean it. I didn't want to apologize. Why do I even have to apologize? That was my revenge. Or so I thought.

"No, don't be sorry. I'm the one who should be apologizing to you. Not you. Never you, Al."

He stares down at the floor.

"Well, here's your chance. What do you want to say?" I say, crossing my arms.

"Shit happens, Al. And shit happened to me when we were together. I regretted it so much, and when I didn't have the balls to tell you, I left you. And I regretted that more than ever."

A headache comes on, throbbing at my temples.

"What happened, Roy?" I ask, even though I already know what's coming.

He takes a couple of sips and clears his throat.

"I had a," he says, and clears his throat again. "I had a one night stand with a stranger. I don't even know how it all happened, but it did. By the time it was over, I knew it meant that you and I were over. I knew that admitting it to you would mean I would lose you. Either way, I would lose you. So, I left you instead and opted to never tell you what happened." He manages to look me in the eye the entire time.

"Thanks for letting me know. But you have to understand that it doesn't change anything now," I say.

"I know that. But I was hoping it would at least change your mind about me. I want you to remember me as the guy who loved you too much to hurt you, not the asshole who simply left. There was more to what happened than just a random breakup. I made a mistake—a huge error that I know I can never undo. And I will never forgive myself for it," he says, with a break in his voice.

I sit quietly, battling my thoughts and my headache. I look at Roy, and I see a guy who is hurting, asking me for forgiveness. I appreciate the gesture, but his apology is not going to save what's left of us.

"Say something, Al," he says.

It takes me a second to react. "I'm going to make some coffee," I reply, rising slowly from my seat. I have nothing left to say.

He takes a few more sips of his wine and follows me.

"Do you need help?" he asks.

"No. Would you like some coffee?"

"Sure," he says, and goes back on the couch.

I force myself to stand up straight and pretend I'm not as intoxicated as I am. I watch the coffee brew and keep my eyes on the machine until it is done. Then I grab our mugs and fill them halfway. Roy gets up and approaches me.

"I'm sorry I hurt you. If I could go back and change things I would, but I can't. All I can do now is apologize, and I know it's not enough. But I hope it's still worth something," he says, standing in my way. I hand him a mug.

"And all I can do is accept your apology. It's all in the past now, Roy. You and I are no longer together, so what does it even matter now?"

My head throbs even more. I take a few sips of my coffee and walk to my orange chair, while Roy goes to the couch. And for a while, we stay quiet.

I check the time. It's past midnight. Roy's thirty minutes is up, but I decide to let him finish his coffee. He takes slow sips with his head down low, grasping the sides of the mug. When he rests it on the coffee table, I blurt, "Roy, you should go."

He nods, his head still down.

I get up and move toward the door. Roy follows.

"Can I at least help you with the dishes?" he asks.

"No, I'm fine."

I know he's stalling.

"Happy Valentine's Day, Al."

I chuckle darkly. "It's past midnight, Roy. Valentine's Day is over. It's been over." I hurry past him and prop the door open. "Goodnight, Roy."

He nods. "Tell Cindy I said congratulations on her wedding. How's Danielle, by the way?" he asks, still stalling.

"She and her husband are expecting their first child," I say, opening the door wider.

"Wow, I can't believe they're both married now."

My heart stops when he says that. Hearing him say it out loud magnifies the fact that I'm still alone. A sense of panic comes over me, and I gasp for air.

I glance at Roy, my vision hazy, and my heart heavy.

"Are you OK, Al?" he says, shutting the door and rushing toward me.

"I'm dizzy," I mutter.

"You need to sit down." He takes me back to the couch, with his arm around my waist, supporting me. We sit, a little too close that our shoulders rub up against each other.

"Can I get you some water?" he asks. I nod.

Roy bolts to the kitchen, comes back with a glass of water, and hands it to me. I take a couple of sips and hand it back to him, and he rests it on the coffee table.

"Better?" he asks.

"A little," I reply.

But I'm not better. My head is cloudy, and I can't think straight.

He lightly rubs my back, and for some reason, it comforts me, to the point where I don't want him to stop. But he stops, and he reaches out and touches my face with the back of his hand. I want so much to push him away, but a part of me doesn't want him to leave. And in my drunken state, I gaze into his eyes and hesitantly rest my hand on his. Confused and lonely, I let corrupt thoughts ruin me. I obsess about how much I fear growing old alone. In my heart, I know I want someone else—someone else I cannot have. But what if there is no one else, and this is it, and I'm stuck with Roy? I hang on to this thought, and use whatever alcohol is left in my veins as an excuse to be vulnerable and stupid. I pretend I still have feelings for Roy and pretend we are made for each other. I could taste the mistake before I even take a bite. As sickening as this makes me feel, I move in closer, and Roy doesn't miss a beat. He kisses me, and I kiss him back.

But I don't feel a thing.

Not a single thing.

Around five in the morning, I wake up next to Roy in my bed, but we're fully clothed. Seeing him lying here makes me realize that having him in my bed isn't going to fill the hole in my heart.

It's the first time I have ever felt so alone.

I sneak out of the room, my heart filled with guilt about last night. I sit on the couch, hating myself as if I had cheated on Jean-Luc, even though Jean-Luc and I aren't together.

Minutes later, I leave Roy a note on the coffee table: *I can't give you what you want. I'm sorry.*

I hurry out in the cold with my sweats, a black wool coat, sneakers, and a heavy scarf wrapped around my neck. I cross the street and order coffee from the café. I sit by the window, taking small sips, while I wait for Roy to leave my apartment.

At exactly 7:37 a.m., I see Roy exit my building completely disheveled. I keep my eyes on him until I can no longer see him, and I hurry back home, pull the sheets off the bed, shove them inside a garbage bag and rush down the hallway and throw it down the chute. I go back to my apartment and sit on my naked mattress, hating myself all over again. When I get up, I notice a napkin on my side table. It's a note from Roy. It says:

Al—I'm sorry, too.

This was it.

This was our closure.

42

The Wrong that Made the Right

In the midst of clearing my dishes, my phone rings.

It's Cindy.

"Hey," I greet.

"You don't sound happy to hear from me. What's wrong?" she asks, concerned.

"I did something last night." I exhale. "Roy was here," I blurt, moving the last of the dishes into the dishwashing rack.

"What! Why was he there? Did he sleep over? What the hell happened last night?" She pauses to sigh. "Lana, did you sleep with him?"

Did I? I'm pretty sure we didn't have sex. I would have remembered.

"No, I didn't. I mean, yes. Well, no. I didn't have sex with him, but he slept over," I say, leaning back on the kitchen counter.

"How did all this even happen?" she asks, baffled.

"I don't know. He was waiting for me when I got home, begging me to let him up. I guess I felt bad for him, and I was tipsy, to say the least, so I let him up."

"Oh, Lana. Why go back?" she says, sounding disappointed.

"I didn't go back!" I say, raising my voice. "I'm not going back," I continue, now in a normal tone. "You don't know how much I'm regretting all this right now. I told him I don't want to get back together. He had this crazy idea that we were."

"Well, you let him up. Did you kiss him?"

I cringe. I don't need to hear my mistakes being repeated back to me.

"Yes, but again, I didn't want to. I was confused last night… and lonely. Alcohol and loneliness is not a good combination. I know that now."

"Sounds like you could use some company."

"Don't come over. I'd rather go out," I say.

"Well, you're in luck. I called because we're having a post-wedding breakfast. Danielle can't make it, but I thought maybe you'd want to join us."

"Yes, I'll go. Where is it?" I ask, desperately.

"It's still at the Waldorf."

"OK. I'll be there soon," I say, rushing Cindy off the phone.

I am sitting at a table full of strangers from Cindy's wedding. I have a plate full of pastries and fruit in front of me, which I haven't touched. I can't stop feeling guilty about what happened last night, and at the same time, I can't stop thinking about Jean-Luc.

"How are you doing over here?" Cindy asks, resting her hand on my shoulder.

"OK. Are you still busy doing your rounds?" I ask, desperate for her attention.

"Yes, but you're my next stop. Walk with me," she says.

I pull the napkin off my lap and toss it over my plate.

"I'm sorry, I can't eat," I say.

"It's OK," Cindy says, wrapping her arm around me. "How are you feeling?"

"Not great," I say, shaking my head.

"Listen, I want you to know that I wasn't judging you this morning."

"I know," I nod. "Don't worry about Roy. It's all over. It's been over."

"How's everything else?" she asks, as we pass the buffet tables.

Just as I am about to reply, Ben rushes over to us.

"Sorry, Lana. I need to steal my wife back for a family picture."

"She's all yours," I say, smiling. "Congratulations again, guys."

"Thank you," they reply in chorus, as their hands meet.

"Is it OK if I go? I have to unpack and run some errands."

"Sure. I'll call you tonight," Cindy says, while Ben pulls her away.

As they disappear into the crowd, I head for the nearest exit.

43

The Bookstore

As I plod down the sidewalks, I think about love and relationships—the present, the past, the future relationships. What makes them all different, and yet, all the same? The beginning of a relationship is always exciting, and the end of the relationship is always depressing.

Seeing Cindy get married to the man of her dreams and seeing Danielle about to have her first child with the love of her life is pretty amazing. I still remember when we were all single, and they dated all the wrong guys. There were a lot of tears shed and lessons learned. They made mistakes. Mistakes they had to go through to get to where they are now. It was part of the journey of growing up and of finding love. True love. Most of the time, you have to make a few mistakes before you get it right.

And then there's me. Still making a lot of mistakes. Was I also with all the wrong guys? Or maybe they were right, but only right for that particular time in my life. Those were my relationships, and then, there was Jean-

Luc. I don't know what to call what we had, but I know for sure that it was pretty spectacular. And as much as it hurts to think about how it all ended, I can never forget how it all began. No, it wasn't a fairy tale, but it was darn close to one.

A few minutes later, I spot a bookstore on 31st W and 57th Street. I know that being surrounded by books will remind me of Jean-Luc, and a part of me craved exactly that.

After grabbing a novel, I park myself on the floor facing the fiction section. I bury my face in a book I've read many times before. A little girl walks over and sits next to me with a picture book in her hand. She holds it close to her face and says out loud, "Brown Bear, Brown Bear, What Do You See?" She pauses to look at me. I put my book down and give her my attention.

"Hi," I greet, with a smile.

"Hi. My mom said I could read out loud here because this is not a library."

"She's right," I say, nodding.

"What are you reading?" she asks.

I lift the book up and show her the cover of The Sun Also Rises.

"Is it a picture book?"

I shake my head.

"Then I can't read it," she says, resting her book on her lap.

I chuckle.

"How old are you?" I ask.

"I'm five, but I'll be six next month. How old are you?" she asks.

"I'm thirty-four," I say.

"I can't count that high yet," she says.

I laugh.

"Who are you here with?" I ask.

"My mom and my little brother. Who are you with?"

"No one," I say.

"Oh." She wrinkles her forehead. "Why are you alone?"

"I just am," I say, shrugging my shoulders.

"You look sad. Are you sad?" she asks, studying me.

I force a smile. "A little," I whisper.

"Why are you sad?" she says, turning her body to face me.

"I can't tell you. It's a secret," I whisper again.

"Oh," she says, furrowing her eyebrows.

"If I tell you why I'm sad, will you tell me why you're sad?"

"You're sad, too?" I ask.

"Yes."

"Why are you sad?"

"I'm sad because you're sad."

My heart melts when she says that.

"Oh, you don't have to be sad because I'm sad."

"So, you still won't tell me why you're sad?"

I chuckle and scoot closer to her. "OK, I'll tell you. But you promise not to tell anyone, right?"

She sits up erect, her eyes sparkling. "I promise."

"OK." I take a deep breath. "I'm sad because I miss someone."

"Is it your grandma? Because I miss my grandma all the time," she says.

I meant to make up something, but "I miss a boy," quickly slips out of my mouth.

Her forehead wrinkles. "You miss a boy? Why?" she says, perplexed. "Why would you miss a boy?" she says, crossing her arms.

I laugh. "I just do," I say, knowing my answer isn't good enough.

"Well, if you miss a boy, why don't you call him? When I miss my grandma, I call her and tell her that I miss her and then she comes over and then I'm happy again and then I no longer miss her. It's that simple, really."

I wish it were that simple. "I want to tell him, but I can't."

"Why not?"

"I can't call him because I don't know his phone number."

"Well, that's a problem." She shakes her head and contemplates for a while. Then she sticks her arm out and waves at me and says, "I got it! Why don't you visit him?"

"I wish I could, but I can't."

"Why not? You don't have his address?" she asks, sighing.

I laugh again. "Well, that, plus, I don't think he wants to see me."

Her shoulders slump. "How do you know he doesn't want to see you?"

"I just know," I say, tightening my lip.

"Oh," she says, staring at her feet, trying to process what I had told her. "That is sad," she finally says.

"Yup," I say, nodding.

"Maybe you should stop missing the boy, so you could stop being sad."

I could tell she is taking my problem quite seriously and is doing her best to help. A five-year-old is giving me advice on boys and feelings. I can't decide whether it's adorable or pathetic.

"I'll try to do that," I say.

She looks up at me and curls her little lips. "Well, you shouldn't be sad anymore anyway."

"Why is that?"

"Because I'm here."

I smile. "Thanks for being here," I say, nudging her lightly with my elbow.

"You're welcome," she says, and scoots back toward the wall and flips the pages of her book, while I return to mine.

Minutes later, her mom and her little brother pick her up, and in no time, I am back to being alone.

44

Dinner at Danielle's

I want to write.

I type up a few sentences, but none of it makes sense. I delete every word and start over, resting my fingers on the keys, waiting for paragraphs to form. But nothing happens. I shut my laptop and phone Danielle. She invites me to have dinner at their place. I hurry and change. I could use the company.

"My life is about to change," Danielle says, folding baby blankets and lining them up on a changing table.

"Are you excited?" I ask, while stowing away baby socks into a small drawer.

"Excited?" she repeats. "I'm more scared than excited. In a matter of weeks, I am going to become a mother, and I have no clue how to do it. It's frightening." She places the blankets inside an empty drawer. "But I will admit, I cannot wait to hold him in my arms and kiss his little hands and feet," she says, smiling.

"I'm sure it will be the best feeling ever. You're going to be a great mother, Danielle."

She smiles at me. "Thanks." She puts her hands on her belly. "I sure hope so."

"Have you guys thought of names yet?"

"Christopher," she says, with a smile.

"Christopher," I repeat.

"It's Ted's father's name, and we like that name a lot," she says.

"I like it, too."

As I watch Danielle arrange all the tiny clothes and toys in the nursery, it makes me wonder if I would or could ever become a mother.

"Let's talk about something else. Let's talk about you. How are you doing?" She glances up at me, "I'm very sorry about Paris, Lana," she says, tilting her head to the side, looking at me, as if my love life is over. It probably is anyway.

"I'm good," I say, trying to sound convincing.

"If you don't want to talk about it, you don't have to," she says.

I sigh. "No, it's fine."

"OK," she says, relieved.

"Why do you think he didn't show up that night?" I ask.

Danielle wobbles to the rocking chair, sits down, and rocks herself.

"This may sound odd to you, but last night, when I couldn't sleep, I kept thinking of all the possible reasons why your Parisian guy stood you up."

I laugh.

"I'm serious," she says.

I shrug. "Well, let's hear it."

She stops rocking and rests her feet on the ottoman in front of her. "I don't think I should tell you."

"Why not?" I say, sitting on the floor.

"Well, you might not like it."

"Just tell me."

"Are you sure?"

"Please tell me."

"OK," she says. "What if he didn't show up because he's with someone else?"

"Wow," I say, rolling my eyes.

"See. I told you."

"No, no. Go on," I say, insisting.

"Maybe he didn't show up because he was trying to break it off with her." She squints her eyes, "Or maybe he wasn't with anyone else, but he saw an old flame that day and they made up."

"Wow, this is terrible," I say, shaking my head.

"Shall I go on?"

"Please do," I say, amused by what I'm hearing.

"Or maybe, he didn't show up because he forgot where your hotel was. And he got lost."

"I can understand *me* getting lost in Paris, but not him. He lives there. He knows his way around," I say, pulling myself up.

"You never know," she says.

"OK, well, thanks for sharing your thoughts, Danielle, but I've heard enough. Let's change the subject," I say, with a dry laugh.

"You're welcome," she says smiling sheepishly, just as Ted arrives.

"Food is here!" he announces, sticking his head inside the nursery.

"Great. I'm starving," Danielle says.

I help her off the rocking chair and follow behind her as she wobbles into the kitchen where a bucket of fried chicken is waiting for us on the counter.

"As requested by my pregnant wife," Ted says, wrapping his arms around Danielle.

"Greasy and good!" she exclaims. "Did you get corn? I want corn. Please tell me you got corn."

"I got corn," he says proudly, and pulls out a container from the bag.

After dinner, Ted makes us ice cream sundaes for dessert. A layer of chocolate sauce over scoops of vanilla ice cream and banana slices fill our bowls. Danielle inhales hers.

An hour later, I help them clear the table and load the dishes into the dishwasher. Soon, Danielle parks herself on the couch and is snoring in no time.

"This happens every night," Ted says, in a loud whisper.

"I should go," I say, grabbing my purse.

"I'll let her know you left," he whispers again.

I nod and walk over to Danielle. I kiss her forehead, skip out the door, and take the subway home.

Half an hour later, I enter my building. I notice a neighbor collecting mail from her mailbox. It reminds me that I haven't checked mine since I've been back. I head over as she leaves. I turn the key to my box and grab the stack of envelopes and catalogs shoved inside.

A minute later, I enter my apartment and leave my mail on the dining table. I shower and change into comfortable clothes and head to the kitchen. As I clear my dishes, I watch the world go by outside my window. On my way to bed, I notice a paper bag on the living room floor. Inside is the notebook I had bought a couple of days ago. I retrieve it from the bag, rush to my room, grab a pen from my dresser, and hop on the bed.

I want to write. I have to write.

I flick the cover off the pen, lay the tip on the first leaf of the notebook, and begin writing.

Go on and search for your fairy tale, if that is what you wish. But do not expect a prince, or a ball, or a castle. Instead, expect a man with an apartment on the second floor in a building with a beautiful courtyard. He will be wearing a wool coat and a scarf hanging loosely around his neck. His eyes will look at you with complete admiration. His smile will melt you away, his voice will soothe you, and his kisses will make your knees weak. Expect your eyes to glow, your heart to dance, your mind to wander, your body to shiver, overwhelmed by this beautiful man that is now yours—but yours temporarily. He will take your breath away, and he will kiss you when you least expect it, and when he does, you will float away into the clouds. He will hold your hand tightly and keep you close, and he will wrap his arms around you when you sleep, while his warm breath sends shivers down your spine. He will make love to you in a room where the light flickers, with books scattered on the floor. You will fall asleep, and hours later, awake in each other's arms. You will make love one more time before the light shines through the window. With your eyes locked on each other, your bodies pressed together, it will feel like nothing could ever come between you. You will fall asleep again and drift away into a dream. Then the sun will rise, and you wake up. And when you open your eyes, your face will be decorated with a smile from last night's bliss. You cannot wait to spend another moment with this man, whose scent has captured you and spun you into a wild state. And suddenly, there you are holding hands in front of your hotel, across the Seine River. He tells you he will see you again in a few hours, and so, you kiss and say goodbye. You sit in your hotel room staring at the clock, counting the hours, the minutes, and the seconds, before you get to see him and hold him again. The time finally arrives, and you wait outside for him as the clock ticks violently and your face has lost its smile. There you stand in your little pretty dress, your eyes welled up with tears, your heart no longer dancing, but your mind wandering and your body shivering from the cold. It is then you realize that there is no fairy tale. Your prince is not coming back. There never was a castle or a happy ever after. Your heart sinks to your knees. Time passes, and you try to move on, but you can't help but dwell on that unforgettable time in Paris, where for a moment, you thought you had it all.

I place my notebook and pen on my side table. My eyes are tired. I'm tired. Tired of everything. Tired of hurting. My head falls back on the soft pillows. I pull the sheets over me and shut my eyes.

It's noon.

I overslept.

I stumble out of bed and drag myself to the bathroom before proceeding to the kitchen to make some coffee. As the coffee brews, I sluggishly approach the dining table. I sit down and notice the stack of mail in front of me.

An envelope catches my eye.

The corner sticks out in red, blue, and white.

I pull it out.

My eyes grow big.

It's an airmail envelope with a stamp that says, *"Par Avion."*

My jaw drops.

It's a letter from Paris.

45

Par Avion

I spring up from my seat, accidentally pushing my chair down causing a loud thump when it hits the ground. I don't pick it up. I take a few deep breaths before ripping the flap open with my fingers. There's a smaller envelope nestled inside. I pull it out. A note is paper-clipped to it.

It reads:

Madame Levine: This letter was left for you late last night, but you had already checked out. We hope to see you again soon.

Best, Josephine

My hands shake as I detach the note from the envelope, and I see my name handwritten in black ink:

Lana.

I dig my index finger through the envelope flap and pull out the folded letter tucked inside. My hands tremble as I unfold the lined paper covered with black ink. I shut my eyes and take another deep breath before I begin to read:

My dear American,

The only way you will understand and possibly forgive me for not showing up that night, is if I reveal the things that I have purposely kept from you. Things I have kept from you, for no other reason than to escape the truth I could not bear to face.

I thought I knew and understood what pain was, what hurt was, what sadness was, until someone very dear to me suddenly passed away a week ago. I was with him at the hospital during his final moments, watching him fade before my eyes. I held his hand until his soul left his body, and it was then that my whole world fell apart. I was heartbroken and devastated, and nothing, not even my life mattered anymore. I forced myself off the floor and left his lifeless body lying peacefully, and I walked the streets until the soles of my shoes grew holes as big as the ones in my heart. But somewhere in the rain, beneath a deluge, I saw you again—the beautiful stranger I had just met the day before. There you were, hiding under your umbrella, crying—sad like I was. I held on to you and found strength in your tears, and in an obscure, and maybe, desperate way, I found happiness within this giant wave of sadness that had buried me so deep. You were that little sparkle in my very dark sky, and my escape from my desolate reality. You were a dream that saved me from a nightmare that was about to ruin me completely. I needed you. You were my distraction, and I wanted to stay in that dream with you and pretend that my life wasn't mine, and that all that ever existed was you and I. But that afternoon, after I dropped you off at your hotel, I went to the wake, and in an instant, I was sucked right back into my reality. And I fell apart all over again. I couldn't see you that night because I was too broken, and I needed time to fix me. Forgive me for not telling you what I was going through. I couldn't. I am sorry I made you wait for me that night.

Here is the poem I wrote at the café.
It was about you.

The Rain
Can I ever be more curious about her?
Her eyes glow in the dark and shimmer in the rain
I push aside my melancholy ways
To enter into her terrain
My senseless resistance to love, I withhold
To see what her mysterious kind can bestow
My heart I lift up in her direction
She seems to have a faithful reaction
I think that I may even love her
How could that be when inside I'm shattered?
Crowded and confused the streets remain
Like my emotions under the rain

I am overwhelmed and displaced, lost within this world I am now in. The days I spent with you are all I think of. I often wish those days would repeat itself into a loop, so that I may never be alone again. There is a lot more I still want to tell you, but I will wait until I see you again. Mon amour, *I hope I see you again.*

I'll be here waiting.
3 Rue Mystère, Paris.
Yours,
Jean-Luc

A tear falls down my cheek, and then another and another. In seconds, I am sobbing uncontrollably, clutching the letter in my hand. I'm happy and sad all at the same time. I read the letter one more time, holding on to every word Jean-Luc had written. I rush to the kitchen and push the window open and let the cold New York breeze caress my skin. As the chilly air brushes up against my wet face, I realize what I need to do.

I need to go back to Paris.

Now.

I shut the window and run to my room. I retrieve my laptop from the floor and feverishly search for a direct flight to Paris.

I can't believe I'm doing this again.

But I must do this.

I need to see Jean-Luc.

I book the only direct flight I see leaving JFK at 8:05 p.m. It will get me to Charles de Gaulle Airport at around 9:00 p.m. the following day. I wait for the email confirmation for my e-ticket. When it arrives, I leap off the bed and shove everything back inside my purse. I grab my toiletries and my makeup kit and lay them on the bed. As my heart beats rapidly, I swing my suitcase open. I hurry to the kitchen and sip my coffee. It only makes me even more nervous and more anxious.

I need to talk to someone. Right now.

I get my phone and dial Danielle's number.

"Hello?" answers the other line, but it's not Danielle's voice.

"Ted?"

"Lana?"

"Is Danielle OK?"

"She's in labor. We're on our way to the hospital," he says, in a frantic tone.

"What! Oh, my god," I say, smacking my forehead. "I'll be right there. Which hospital?"

After he tells me the address, I hang up the phone, grab Jean-Luc's letter, and head straight for the door.

46

Baby Christopher

How do I contain myself?

I'm overwhelmed with so many thoughts and emotions. I can't sit still. I can't stop thinking and worrying about Danielle, but I also can't stop thinking about Jean-Luc and his letter.

The cab drops me off at the front of the hospital. I rush out, forcing myself to focus on what's happening right now. *My best friend is about to have a baby.*

I stop by the information desk, and they send me up to the 8th floor, where Danielle's room is located.

"Are you OK?" I greet, the moment I enter Danielle's room. She's wearing a white cotton robe, pink fluffy slippers, and her hair is up in a bun. A nurse helps her off the bed.

"Oh, Lana. I'm so glad you're here," she says, managing a weak smile.

"Of course. Where else would I be?"

Probably at home, packing for Paris.

"Where's Ted?" I ask.

"He stepped out to call my mom to let her know we're here."

The nurse leads her toward the bathroom in small strides.

"Can I help you with anything?" I ask, taking her hand.

"Sure," Danielle says. She turns to the nurse and says, "Thanks, Ruby. Lana can take it from here."

"You're welcome, sweetie," Ruby says then faces me. "Looks like you're in charge now. Keep track of her contractions and call us if you need anything."

"Will do," I say, smiling.

As soon as the nurse leaves the room, I whisper to Danielle, "Sorry, but what exactly is a contraction? What am I supposed to be doing?"

"Probably best that you don't know. Just promise me you'll be close by so I can squeeze your hand when it happens," she says.

I help Danielle back on the bed and stack a bunch of pillows behind her. Then I step out to refill a pitcher with water. As much as I'd want to tell her about the letter from Paris, and the fact that I have a flight to catch in a few hours, I keep my mouth shut. Now is not the time to talk about it or even think about it. Danielle is about to have a baby, and that's all she should be thinking about at the moment.

When I get back to the room, Ted and Diane are already there.

"Hey, Lana," Ted greets, as he massages Danielle's lower back. "I'm glad you called earlier."

"I'm glad I called, too," I say.

"How did you know Danielle was in labor?" Diane asks, as she gives me a hug.

As I'm about to reveal the real reason why I called, I decide to bite my tongue.

"I guess I had a hunch," I say, with a shrug.

"That's why we're best friends," Danielle says proudly, leaning back on her pillows.

"Speaking of best friends, does Cindy know we're all here?" I ask, changing the subject.

"No, please call her," Danielle says, in the midst of doing breathing exercises.

"OK, I'll call her now."

I ring Cindy the moment I exit the room. She picks up the phone after several rings.

"I'm at the hospital. Danielle is in labor," I announce.

"What?" she says, in a loud whisper. "Shit! What time is it? Where is it? I'm on my way," she says, and hangs up the phone before I can even answer any of her questions, so I text the information instead.

I step out to buy some coffee and pastries from the coffee shop in the lobby and bring them up to the room. Danielle's eyes are closed when I enter.

"Is Cindy coming?" she asks, her eyes still shut.

"Yes, she's on her way now. How are you doing?"

"I'll be better once I get an epidural," she says, holding Ted's hand.

Nurse Ruby walks in with the anesthesiologist to give Danielle her epidural. I excuse myself, leave the room, and sit on a chair next to the door. I look down the hallway, my eyes land on the elevator bank. I watch the up and down buttons turn on and off as the doors open and shut, and people walk in and out. *Ding!* The elevator doors open again. This time, Cindy storms out holding a Red Bull, wearing no makeup, burgundy sweats, and running shoes. She speeds down the hallway, with her brown curly hair flying every which way.

"Did she already have the baby? Did I miss it?" she yells out, from a few feet away.

"No, she didn't. You're fine," I reply, rising from my seat. "Did you just wake up?" I say, hugging her.

"Can't you tell?" she says, laughing. "I was up late planning our itinerary for our honeymoon. By the time I fell asleep, it was already four in the morning."

"Well, you haven't missed the birth," I say, sitting back down.

"I'm glad," she says, catching her breath. "You want some?" she asks, offering me her drink. I decline. "What are you doing out here?" she asks, and takes a few sips of her Red Bull.

"They're giving Danielle an epidural."

"That's good."

"I can't believe they're about to become parents any minute now," I say.

"It's insane. I'm stressing out and I'm not the one having the baby." We laugh.

"Are you all packed for your honeymoon?"

Cindy shakes her head and tosses her drink in the bin across from us. "Not even close. I'm glad the wedding is over. But don't get me wrong. It was the best day of my life, but planning that wedding for an entire year was kind of the worst time of my life," she says, laughing to herself, clearly caffeinated.

"I don't think I'll be planning a wedding anytime soon."

"You never know. It could happen sooner than you think," she says, nudging me with her elbow.

I tighten my lips, wanting to tell her everything, but I hold myself back because talking about my situation now would be selfish. Instead, I feign a smile and nod.

"What's new with you?" she asks, while applying lip balm on her lips.

"With me?" I ask, as if there was any possibility that she could be asking someone else. "Not much." I say, avoiding her eyes.

"Are you sure?" she asks, trying to read me. "Something's off."

"Something's off?" I repeat. "I'm fine. Why?"

"I don't know." She squints her eyes at me.

Before I could say anything else, the door swings open and the nurse and the anesthesiologist exit Danielle's room.

Cindy enters before me, and I trail behind her.

"How are you doing?" she says, rushing over to Danielle's side.

"I'm OK. Thank you for being here. I love you both," Danielle says, smiling weakly.

"Love you, too," Cindy and I say in chorus.

We spend the next couple of hours waiting for the baby to arrive, sitting around chatting, taking turns getting more water and ice. And then, in an instant, everything changes. Nurses walk in, followed by the doctor who speaks to Danielle and instructs his crew.

Danielle is about to become a mom!

As Ted videotapes the momentous event, Cindy and I hold on to Danielle's hands, and we manage to help coach her with her pushing and breathing. She sweats profusely, and somehow, so do we.

"Danielle, I need you to push down. Push, push, push," orders the doctor, in a stern, but calm voice.

Danielle grips our hands and pushes and pushes, then screams and pushes and screams again. This goes on for a while until the doctor announces that a head is coming out. Danielle squeezes our hands even tighter, while Ted grips his camera. Minutes later, a beautiful baby boy pops out. Danielle releases our hands. The second we hear the baby crying, we join him in sobs.

"We did it," Danielle says, weakly.

"No, you did it all," I say, hugging her.

"Congratulations, guys! You have a healthy baby boy!" announces the doctor.

"I have a baby," Danielle says, completely exhausted and in tears. Diane takes the camera from Ted and continues filming. The nurse hands Ted a pair of scissors and he cuts the umbilical cord. The nurses take the baby, clean him up, and wrap him tight in a hospital blanket before handing him to the new father.

Ted rushes over to Danielle's side.

"Congratulations, guys," I say, making way for him and the baby.

"He's beautiful," Cindy says.

"I'm an aunt!" Diane says as she hurries over to see the baby, while still holding the camera and still filming.

"I'm a mom," Danielle says, now cradling the baby in her arms.

"And I'm a dad," Ted says, and kisses her forehead and kisses the baby's forehead. A second later, Danielle's mom enters the room with a giant basket of goodies.

"Danielle, Mom is here! I'm here!" she says, panting.

"Our baby boy has arrived!" Ted announces.

"Oh, I can't believe it. I'm a grandma again!" she says, dropping the basket of goodies on the floor and rushing to her daughter's bedside. She kisses Danielle's cheek and squeezes Ted's hand. With a huge smile on her face, she looks at the baby and says, "My little Christopher. Oh, my little Christopher."

I'm so glad I didn't miss this.

47

Best Friends

A couple of hours later, Cindy and I volunteer to pick up our late lunch. It's 3:30 p.m. On our way out of the hospital, we talk about how amazing it was to have witnessed the birth of Christopher, and how wonderful it was that we were there for Danielle the entire time.

Now that it's all over, and the baby has arrived, and Danielle is recovering smoothly, the anxiety inside of me kicks into full blast. I need to tell Cindy about what's going on or I am going to burst.

We exit the hospital and head down the block to pick up sandwiches from a food truck. After picking up the food, we head back inside and decide to stop by the hospital gift shop.

"Are you getting something?" she says, surveying the store.

"What do you think about this bear?" I say, lifting up a small brown bear with a blue cap on.

"Cute," she says.

"I'll get this one."

"I thought for sure Danielle would give birth during our honeymoon. I'm glad I didn't miss it," Cindy says, approaching a selection of Mylar balloons.

"Yeah, me too," I say, staring blankly at the bear.

"Are you OK?" she says, pausing in front of me.

"Yup," I say, and walk to the register.

"You're not telling me something," she whispers, while I pay for the bear.

I give her a tight smile, and I don't say anything.

But as we leave the gift shop, I blurt out, "Cindy, I need to tell you something."

She turns to me, her eyes squinted. "I knew it," she says and follows me toward the elevators. "I knew something was off."

"Jean-Luc wrote me a letter," I say, as a crowd grows behind us.

"The guy from Paris? Holy shit. He emailed you?" she says, in a loud whisper.

"No, he wrote me an actual letter. He left it at the hotel I was staying at the day I checked out." The elevator doors open. "The hotel mailed me the letter," I finish.

"Hold on. Let's take the next one," she says, pulling me to the side. "Wait, they didn't tell him you already checked out?" she says, shaking her head.

"No, they didn't. But I don't think he gave them a chance to. He probably just walked in, left the letter at the front desk, and walked out."

I can tell from the expression on Cindy's face that what I was about to say was going to baffle her. "This is probably going to sound a bit impulsive, but this morning, I booked a flight to Paris."

"What?"

"Look, I know this all sounds crazy, and I don't expect you to understand any of it. But something in my gut and in my heart, is telling me that I need to go back to Paris now. And it's not just about the letter. It's beyond the letter. I want to see Jean-Luc again. I need to see him again. Am I crazy?" I say, my heart racing.

She looks at me and says in a calm tone, "Did you bring the letter?"

I reach inside my purse and hand her the envelope.

She takes it, grabs my hand, and leads me outside where we find a bench on the side of the building. She sits down, pulls out the letter, and unfolds it. "I can't believe it's handwritten," she says, under her breath.

I watch her read the letter, her eyes focused, quickly moving down the page. When she finishes, she looks up at me and sighs a dreamy sigh.

"Oh, Lana," she says, and folds the letter carefully and hands it back to me.

"What do you think of the letter?" I say, tucking the letter inside the envelope and slipping it back in my purse.

She smiles and doesn't say anything. It only makes me more anxious.

"Oh, Lana," she says again, her face softening.

"What do you think? Is it crazy for me to go back to Paris?" I say, struggling to remain still.

"Sure, it's crazy. But isn't that what love is? Love is fucking nuts. Half the time, we end up doing things with our eyes closed, and that's how we make mistakes. But we also do the right things. And once in a while, we do something that's just right, and it makes all the difference. You going back to Paris might be that one thing that you get just right." She shrugs her shoulders. "I get it, Lana. Trust me, I've done some crazy shit in my life, and I'm glad I have." She pauses. "Sometimes crazy is good, and you have to do it. Sometimes it's the only way you'll get answers."

My face relaxes, and my heart rate returns to normal. It turns out, it was a good idea to tell Cindy after all.

"By the way, that's a damn good letter." She puts her hand on mine. "Go to Paris, Lana. Go see your man."

I hug her tight, my eyes watering. "Thanks, Cindy. I will."

"We should probably take their lunch up now," Cindy suggests.

"That's a good idea," I say, pushing back my tears.

Cindy gets up, and we proceed toward the hospital doors.

"Does Danielle know about all this?"

"No, she doesn't. I was about to tell her this afternoon when I called. But that's when Ted picked up and told me she was in labor. And that's when I rushed here."

"It's been quite a day, hasn't it?"

"Yes, it has," I say, as we squeeze inside the elevator with a crowd of doctors.

"Let's not tell Danielle about all this right now. It wouldn't be right. I want it to be all about baby Christopher," I whisper to Cindy.

"OK," she says.

"Danielle's going to be a great mom," I say.

"Yes, she is."

48

Changes

It's only Ted, Danielle, and Christopher when we get back in the room. Danielle is breastfeeding the baby.

"Lunch is here," Cindy announces, placing the food on the table.

"Thanks, guys," Danielle says.

"Here's a little bear for Christopher," I say, resting the stuffed toy on the foot of the bed.

"That's very sweet. Thank you," Danielle says.

"How's the breastfeeding going?" Cindy asks.

"He wouldn't latch on at first, but I think we're both getting the hang of it."

"That's good," Cindy says, getting comfortable on a chair. A nurse comes in and talks to Danielle for a while. She helps her clean up the baby and move him back to his crib.

After lunch, Ted steps out to make a few phone calls. When the door shuts behind him, I catch a glimpse of the clock by the door and realize the time.

My body tenses up.

If I don't leave soon, I will miss my flight.

As I get restless in my seat, Danielle and Cindy talk about how everyone's lives are changing. Danielle and Ted are parents now, and Cindy and Ben are married.

"So true," I say, glancing up at the clock, clenching my jaw.

"Lana's life is changing, too," Cindy blurts. I snap my head toward her. She gives me a funny look, as if hinting for me to say something.

"What do you mean?" Danielle asks.

"Oh, um, Craig said that a major publisher loved my last article and might offer me a book deal." I swallow hard.

Cindy's eyes widen. "What?"

"That's such great news, Lana," Danielle says.

"Congratulations," Cindy says, glaring at me.

"Hey, Cindy. Can I talk to you quickly in the bathroom?"

Cindy nods and follows me. I push her in and pull the door.

"Hey, is that true about the book deal? If it is, that's fantastic. Why didn't you tell me sooner?" Cindy says.

"Yes, it's true." I shake my head at her. "I thought we weren't going to mention anything about Paris?"

"I know, I'm sorry, but it's the three of us. It seemed like a good time to tell her. Besides, you looked like you wanted to say something."

"I do want to say something." I say, in a loud whisper.

"About the book deal or about Paris?"

"About Paris."

"What is it?"

"My flight leaves soon."

She looks at me closely and sees the panic in my face.

"Lana, how soon is soon?"

"In three hours."

"What the hell are you still doing here?" she says out loud, and kicks the bathroom door open. "You have to leave now!"

"*Ssshh!*" I say, grabbing the door.

"You need to catch your flight, Lana," Danielle yells out.

"Great," I say, under my breath, rolling my eyes at Cindy.

She shrugs her shoulders, while we exit the bathroom. I saunter over to Danielle, while Cindy plops down on a chair, looks at Danielle and says, "I'll fill you in later. Lana has to go."

"I'm sorry, Danielle. I didn't want to say anything."

"Why not? Because I had a baby?"

"Yes. It didn't feel right to bring it up. This is your day, and I wish I could stay longer and be here for you."

"Don't be silly. Lana, you've done more than enough. You guys were here for the most important part, and I'm so thankful for that. I'm fine. He's fine. Look at him sleeping peacefully. He doesn't know what's going on." We share a laugh. "Besides, today is our day, not only mine. Our lives are all changing, remember?" Danielle says, sitting up.

"Lana, why are you still here? Go!" Cindy orders.

"OK," I say, frozen in my spot. "I can't believe I'm doing this," I say, my heart racing, my mind going wild.

"Go!" Danielle says.

"Go find Jean-Pierre," Cindy says, getting up.

"His name is Jean-Luc," Danielle corrects her, with a chuckle.

"Oh, whatever," Cindy says. We all laugh as my eyes well up with tears.

I hug Danielle and blow a kiss at baby Christopher. Cindy is already holding the door open for me with my purse in her hand. I take my purse and give her a tight hug and run toward the elevator.

49

The Flight

After ten minutes of sitting in traffic, I ditch the cab and run the 11 blocks home. By the time I get to my apartment, it is already 6:00 p.m. I shower, change, and ring Fred, the doorman, and ask him to call me a cab. Five minutes later, I zip up my suitcase and bolt out the door. At exactly 6:30 p.m., I hop in the cab that is already waiting for me, and we head straight to JFK Airport.

An hour later, the cab swerves into the airline curb. I haul out my belongings and run inside. I check in then hurry to security. It's past 7:30 p.m. My flight is already boarding. Twenty minutes later, I pass security. I collect my purse and jacket from the plastic bin, move to a bench, and shove my feet back inside my boots. I check my ticket for the gate number. It's 38, which happens to be the last one. I weave through the crowd, running past the terminals, praying that my flight hasn't left yet. But as I approach, I notice it's empty, except for the gate agent who is getting ready to shut the doors.

"Wait! Please wait!" I yell out, sprinting toward her.

She raises her hands up in the air and gestures for me to hurry up. When I arrive at the gate, I thank her multiple times, while catching my breath. She scans my boarding pass and says, "Welcome to Air France," in a calm, nasally voice. I thank her one last time and rush down the ramp and board the plane.

Everyone has settled in. I quickly locate my seat in the middle of the plane. An older man is sitting by the window with his headphones on and an eye mask. The middle seat is empty, and I have the aisle seat. I sit down, tuck my purse under the seat in front of me and fasten my seatbelt. The flight attendants make their final check, and within minutes, we are taxiing on the runway.

I reach inside the seat pocket for headphones. I put them on and surf the stations until I hear a French song playing. Perfect. I increase the volume and press my head against my chair and close my eyes.

I feel a strong nudge on my elbow. My eyes snap open. A flight attendant pushing her cart looks back at me and apologizes, then turns around and continues down the aisle. I take off my headphones and sit up. A baby laughs. I glance over at my row mate who is snoring away with his head against the window. I hear the baby laugh again and notice him one row down, smiling and holding onto his mother's hands, his chubby legs wobbling on her lap. The baby sees me looking at him and smiles. The mother looks back, sees me, and also smiles.

"He's adorable," I say, smiling back.

"Thank you," she says, and turns her attention back at her baby.

I watch the mother grab the diaper bag from under the seat with one hand, while holding the baby with the other. She pulls out a bottle of formula and shakes it, as the baby hangs onto his mother's arms. The mother opens the formula and attaches a nipple to the top. She lays the baby down, his head resting on her arm. She tilts the bottle and gets him drinking in no time. She watches him with a loving smile, while he looks up at her, his eyes glistening. It reminds me of Danielle and her baby and how strong and brave Danielle was. Could I ever be or would I ever be as brave as her, or any other mother out there? The thought alone frightens me.

I look out the window to distract myself, watching the fluffy clouds float around us. I focus on Paris and Jean-Luc. Goosebumps fill my body. I shut the window shades and try to calm myself down. As I take slow deep breaths, a flight attendant stops by and asks me if I want a drink.

Yes. I need one. Desperately.

"I'll have a glass of red wine, please," I reply.

Minutes later, I order another.

50

Paris

The alcohol knocks me out for hours. When I wake up, I catch the tail end of the announcement.

"Flight attendants, prepare for landing."

My heart beats faster as the plane descends into Paris. Unable to keep still I sit forward and backward, and I peek out the window and do it all over again.

I lean back in my chair with my eyes now closed, clutching the sides of my seat. I inhale slowly and exhale.

Minutes later, our plane hits the runway and jolts us. I hold on tighter, my insides turning, and my heart racing. I check the time obsessively as we taxi the runway. The plane finally stops. When the seatbelt light turns off, I let go of my seat, my hands drenched with sweat. It's 9:15 p.m.

I search for the closest restroom the minute we deplane. I freshen up, head to baggage claim, speeding past my fellow passengers. It takes me over an hour to get my suitcase and pass customs. When I exit the airport doors,

I rush to the cab line, which is short, and in minutes, I'm reading out Jean-Luc's address to the cab driver. I stow the letter back inside my purse. While my heart pounds at an unusual speed, I fix my eyes on the scenery of trees and buildings that speed past us. I can't believe I'm back. I can't wait to see Jean-Luc.

As we drive along Saint-Germain-des-Prés, it's like I'm flipping through pages of a memory book. We make a left on Saint-Michel and drive past the Shakespeare and Company bookstore to the right, and past Notre Dame Cathedral to the left. Minutes later, we cruise along a street I don't recognize.

"Excuse me, Monsieur? Are we getting close?" I ask.

"Oui, Madame," he replies.

My heart thumps loudly. I reach inside my purse for my wallet, as the cab pulls up to a curb.

I look up and gasp.

My heart stops.

This isn't Jean-Luc's apartment building.

"I'm sorry, why did you stop here?" I ask, my throat drying up.

"This is your destination, *Madame,"* he says, looking at me through the rear-view mirror.

My destination?

"No, no, this is a mistake," I say, yanking out the letter from my purse and reading out the address to him one more time.

"Oui," he says, nodding. "3 Rue Mystère," he repeats and points at the building in front of us. "Le Café Dubois," he says.

I glance at the address on the letter and look up at the café. I repeat this several times until I make myself dizzy. The driver taps on the meter to remind me that it's time to pay my fare. I pay him, my hands moving in slow motion. Befuddled, I exit the cab. He gets out and drops off my suitcase on the pavement and drives away.

My knees tremble as I look around me. The alley is dark and quiet. The only thing I can hear is my own heart beating in my chest. I look down and notice that all the flowers and cards that were here weeks ago have disappeared. I drag my suitcase toward the door.

A small sign on the wall confirms I am indeed at the right address: *3 Rue Mystère*.

But what am I doing here?

I check the door. No padlock and no note.

Before fear sets in, I push the door with my hands shaking.

It opens.

My heart thumps.

Chills rush through my body, as I walk past the red velvet curtains.

The café is empty except for two waiters busy stacking chairs. Soft music plays in the background.

"Hello? Do you speak English?" I blurt, gripping the handle of my suitcase.

"Bonsoir, Madame. Sorry, we are closed," says one of the waiters.

"Can we help you?" says the other waiter, who is taller than the other.

"I'm supposed to meet someone here." I swallow hard.

They look at each other.

"We are the only ones here," the shorter waiter explains.

"This café was closed a few weeks ago," I say, ignoring what he had just said.

"*Oui*, it was closed," says the taller waiter, as he pauses from stacking chairs. "But only for a few weeks in honor of *Monsieur Dubois.*"

"Yes, I know," I mumble, scanning the place, my eyes darting from one side of the room to the other, recalling the day I came in here weeks ago and saw the matchmaker.

"Did you know *Monsieur Dubois?*" the shorter waiter asks.

"I knew of him." I pause. "When did the café reopen?"

"Last week," they reply in chorus.

"His grandson reopened it last week," says the taller one.

"Grandson?" I ask.

"*Oui*, his grandson," confirms the same waiter as I catch a glimpse of an old black and white photo hanging above the door.

It's a photo of an old man next to a little boy. My gaze rests on the photo. I can't stop looking at it, my eyes glued to the little boy. I keep staring at his face, straining my eyes on the grainy, faded image.

"Do you know Jean-Luc?" asks one of the waiters.

My heart stops.

Did he say, Jean-Luc? Surely, Jean-Luc is a common name here, right? It can't be the same Jean-Luc that I know.

"Jean-Luc?" I repeat, my throat drying up.

"*Oui*, the grandson. The boy in the photo," says the taller waiter, pointing above the door.

"The boy? Grandson?" I say, slurring my words. My head tilts back, and I stare at the photo one more time, my heart racing as it suddenly hits me.

The little boy is the Jean-Luc that I know.

All of a sudden, everything becomes hazy, and I lose my balance, but manage to grab the edge of the table closest to me.

"Are you OK, *Madame?*" asks one of the waiters, I have lost track of which one. Everything becomes a blur, and my ears clog up. Within minutes, a glass of water appears in front of me, and I am scooped up and plopped on a chair. I manage to take a few sips of water with one of the waiters holding the glass for me.

Soon I hear, "Are you OK, *Madame?*" A line repeated to me several times in the midst of them chattering in French.

I can hear myself breathing hard and heavy, as my vision slowly returns. I raise my head and see both waiters standing in front of me with worried looks.

"I'm fine. Thank you," I say, in a weak voice. I force myself to straighten up in my seat.

"You can stay for a while," says the taller waiter.

"Thank you very much," I say, managing a smile.

While I sit here watching the waiters finish stacking the chairs, all I can think about is Jean-Luc and the matchmaker and how they're related.

But how could this be?

Soon the music stops, and the waiters tell me it's time to go. I thank them for their hospitality and they apologize for having to send me away. I collect my suitcase and purse and we exit the café together. My chest hurts as the doors shut behind us. I step off the sidewalk and watch the waiters saunter down the dark alley. When I can no longer see them, I pull my suitcase. In no hurry, I trudge down the alley, listening to the wheels of my suitcase as they rumble loudly like the thoughts in my head. A minute later, I pause to look back at the café. No matter how hard I try to look away, I can't. Jean-Luc is the matchmaker's grandson. I can't fathom the thought. And out of nowhere, a cold breeze blows and covers my body, making every part of me shiver. Then it all goes away as quickly as it came.

I take a deep breath and turn around. As I step forward, a familiar voice stops me.

"American. Wait!"

51

Jean-Luc

I spin around, my knees trembling, my heart racing.

Jean-Luc is a few feet away from me, wearing a black coat, dark pants, and a loose scarf wrapped around his neck.

"I read your letter," I manage to say, my throat dry.

"You're here," he says, a weak smile on his face. He moves toward me, and when he gets closer, I notice dark circles around his eyes.

"Oh, Jean-Luc," I say, my eyes watering. "I had no idea *Monsieur Dubois* was your grandfather."

"He was my only family. He was my best friend," he says, tightening his lips.

I take a few steps closer. "All that time you were comforting me, when I should've been comforting you." I pause as a tear rolls down my cheek. "I'm so, so, sorry, Jean-Luc. I really am," I say, now choking in my tears. He rushes to my side and wipes my wet face with his hands like he's done before. He wraps his arms around me, and I hold him tight.

"I wanted to see you that night, and I planned to. But when I was at my grandfather's wake, my…"

I cut him off. "You don't need to explain. I read the letter," I say, pulling him even closer.

"My mother was there. For the first time in more than a decade, I saw my mother."

I release him. His eyes are focused on the ground, his hair blowing in the wind.

"Oh, Jean-Luc," I say, knowing how hard it must have been for him to see his mother after all these years, especially seeing her at his grandfather's wake.

He looks at me for a quick second before his eyes drop to the ground.

"She looked nothing like I remembered her. She was tiny. She hugged me with her thin arms, and I hugged her back, thinking the entire time that I had my arms around a stranger. Possibly a distant relative I had never met before. I had no idea who she was until she spoke, and I heard her familiar voice. I couldn't believe it was her." He pauses. "She told me how sorry she was for leaving me and how sorry she was about my grandfather. I couldn't even respond. I stood there in awe of what was in front of me and what was happening inside my heart and what was going through my mind."

I reach for his hand.

"All the resentment I've had for her all these years dissolved right there and then." He shrugs and says, "I was no longer mad. I was just sad. I felt compassion for her. Yes, I lost my best friend, my grandfather, but she had lost her father." He looks up at me and continues, "After the wake, my mother and I went back to my grandfather's house. We talked for hours, and in the midst of us catching up, she apologized repeatedly. I begged her to stop, but I could see that it somehow eased her pain, so I did the only thing that made sense—I let her. That was around the time I was supposed to see you." He inhales deeply. "But there was no way I could leave. I was with my mother, and as much as I wanted to see you, Lana, she needed me, and at that moment, I needed her."

I simply nod and continue to listen.

Jean-Luc tells me he stayed with his mother at his grandfather's house that night because it was the right thing to do. The next few days they cleaned out his grandfather's home and discovered old photographs and found one of him and her from the first year they moved to Paris. He tells me about the picture, describing his short-sleeved button-down shirt and gray shorts and his black shoes which were enormous on him. When his mother sees the photo, she cries and apologizes all over again. He says it was hard seeing her in that state. As angry as he might have been with her all these years, he never wanted to see her that way. He wanted her to stop punishing herself for what she had done to him. But the guilt inside her had eaten her up, making her frail. He told her he had forgiven her and was happy they were finally together, but this only made her apologize a few more times. A few days later, she cried less and apologized less, and they began to have normal conversations. As normal as they could be.

"I was with my mother," he says, his voice breaking. "I never thought I would ever see her again."

I lean my head on his shoulder. "I can only imagine what you went through," I say, hoping I could have said more, but I don't know what else to say.

"I couldn't tell you about my grandfather because I didn't want you to feel sorry for me. I had just met you the day before he passed away. The last conversation I had with him before I found out he was very ill, was about you." He looks at me. "He asked about you."

"About me?" I say, as goose bumps fill my entire body.

"The day you came to the café, he saw me looking at you from the bar, and when you left, he watched me run for the door. He smiled at me like he's never smiled at me before. It was as though he knew what I was thinking, or what I wanted to do," he explains.

"Wait, you were there?" I ask, breathless.

"Yes, I was," he says.

"What did you want to do?"

"Follow you, see you, talk to you," he says, looking into my eyes.

Jean-Luc proceeds to tell me that when I walked away from him on the bridge—on the day we first met, a strange feeling came over him. He felt like his life was about to change, but he didn't know how or when. He went back to the café and told his grandfather about me during dinner and a few glasses of wine. He said his grandfather smiled widely upon hearing our story and rested his hand on his shoulder and told him he was happy to hear that. About an hour later, his grandfather collapsed on the kitchen floor. Jean-Luc rushed him to the hospital. It was then that he found out that his grandfather had been ill. His heart had been too weak for a very long time. Jean-Luc says it wasn't until after he had passed that he realized why his grandfather appeared so happy when he told him about me. All these years Jean-Luc had given up on love, and all these years his grandfather did everything he could to show Jean-Luc why he should never give up on love. His grandfather spent all this time matching strangers. Couples he had matched would come back, weeks, months, even years later and thank him for his gift. And his grandfather would tell him about it, but Jean-Luc would always brush off their praises with his cold heart. He said that all his grandfather ever wanted was for him to experience one day what they had. Just once. When he told him about me, he said his grandfather's eyes sparkled, because he saw there was hope. He believed that maybe, Jean-Luc's cold, closed heart had slightly opened. Even a little bit. And this brought extreme joy to his grandfather.

Jean-Luc raises his head and stares up at the skies . "I miss him terribly," he says.

"I know you do," I say, squeezing his hand.

"I'm sorry I didn't tell you about him sooner. I just couldn't. My world had suddenly collapsed, and all I wanted was a distraction—something to keep me from falling apart. When I saw you the day he passed away, I thought for sure I had lost my mind. Because how else could you have appeared like that? But everything became real when I got close to you and saw you crying and I touched your face and felt your tears beneath my fingers. Somehow that gave me strength and made me realize I wasn't alone. Someone else was sad and broken like I was." He looks at me. "You saved me," he says.

I, saved him? But how could I have saved him when all I had with me was a cracked and brittle heart that longed to be loved?

As I slowly digest Jean-Luc's words, my empty heart becomes full.

"I don't know why, but something about being with you feels right. And I can't explain it," he says.

I want to tell him I know exactly what he means, but I don't. Instead, I say, "Maybe sometimes, the best things in life are the things we can't explain and the things we can't understand. Maybe they don't make sense because they don't have to." After I say this, I get the urge to tell him about the magazine article and how I ended up in Paris in the first place. But as I contemplate the thought, Jean-Luc pulls out a piece of paper.

My eyes widen when I realize what's in his hand.

It's the magazine article about the matchmaker.

I try to say something—anything, but nothing comes out.

"You dropped this the day we first met," he says, handing it to me. "A lot happened that day that I forgot all about it. Until this morning, when I found it in my coat pocket," he says.

I stare at the article as memories of the last few weeks run through my head, reminding of how and where it all began, and how much my life has changed.

"Believe it or not, this was why I came to Paris." I glance at Jean-Luc. "This little piece of paper gave me hope and sent me here," I say, my eyes wet with tears.

"And when you dropped it, it sent me to you."

Jean-Luc is right. But deep in my soul, I know that something far greater than all of this had brought us to each other. I realize now that sometimes failed plans are disguised as missed opportunities but are meant to take us somewhere magical.

Now it's my turn to give others hope. Hope in love. Hope in life. And at this moment I decide that I will call Craig and tell him I will write that book. And yes, I will write about Paris, the café, and the matchmaker. Maybe from my experience and from my own words, others will find what it is they are looking for. Like I found mine through Sylvia's words.

As I stand here now, beside Jean-Luc, I don't see marriage or kids in our future. All I see is him and I, and it's enough. This is all I ever wanted. To be with him.

"I'm sorry I didn't show up that night," he says, his tone somber and sincere.

I move in closer, his face a few inches from mine. "You don't ever have to apologize again, because it's not necessary." I take his hands and firmly squeeze them. "Besides, we're together now."

He lifts his head, and when our eyes meet, he breaks a smile on his beautiful melancholy face. It feels as though if I look up at the stars above, they would all be aligned. I want to peek and check if I'm right, but I don't. Instead, I look at Jean-Luc who gazes deep into my eyes, holds my hand, and grips my heart. And as my heart flutters, all I can think of is how much I want to take care of this man. This man standing in front of me whose face I have memorized. I want to take care of him. I've never felt this way about anyone before.

When my thoughts drift into a blissful stream, Jean-Luc kisses my lips, and I kiss him back. Right here, right in front of Le Café Dubois, on a clear night, minutes before midnight, right under the dark Paris sky.

The End

Did you enjoy reading
Hearts and Errors?

Leave a review on Amazon and/or Goodreads!
Share your thoughts on social media using the following
hashtags: #heartsanderrorsanovel #coreymp

Other titles by Corey M.P.
HIGH (A Caffeinated Love Story)

Available on www.amazon.com
www.barnesandnoble.com

ACKNOWLEDGMENTS

I cannot think about the beginnings of this novel without remembering and recognizing the hurdles I faced the year I wrote the first draft—none of which had anything to do with the writing process.

Writing a novel is difficult and rewarding. But nothing is more difficult and more rewarding than being a mom. You worry and love more than you ever thought you were capable of. At times, it may take everything you've got to fight for your child or children, and believe in them—especially when they are born with unique challenges that you, or anyone else, don't, and might not ever understand. And while you swim or tread in this unexpected current, you, as a parent, might begin to lose who you are. I *did.* Until writing brought me back.

In 2009, I left my job as a graphic designer to care fulltime for our daughter who was born with special needs. In 2011, while suffering from a rare chronic pain nerve disorder that sprung up on me, six months after giving birth—I craved writing. I needed it. It was a necessity. Despite dealing with my condition which, by now, had debilitated me, I challenged myself to write a novel in 100 days. In between my daughter's therapy and doctor's appointments, and the chaos that made up my life at the time, I wrote. Five minutes, ten minutes—whatever I had and whenever I could, I wrote. 100 days later, the first draft of HEARTS AND ERRORS was finished. Then it stayed in my computer—untouched, while life happened. By November of 2011, I went through brain surgery for my nerve condition, recovered, and healed. It was liberating and invigorating to be able to speak, eat, drink, and move my mouth and face again—without any pain. I immediately set new goals, published my first novel HIGH (A Caffeinated Love Story), and then created Sammy's Books—a collection of picture books for young children.

Through adversity, I discovered new strength and realized my capabilities. I learned that taking care of my family while pursuing a dream was possible. Creating this book was a labor of love. Writing, editing, and designing the cover and interior were challenges I embraced wholeheartedly. With resilience, hope, and hard work—along with the love, strength, and support of my family and my dear friends, we hold this book in our hands. And for them, I am forever grateful.

To my group of trusted beta readers, Mia, Linda, Kristen, and Erwin, thank you for lending me your time and for your honest and invaluable feedback.

To my mother, Elenita who read the first draft of Hearts and Errors and fell in love with the story, thank you for always believing in me. And to my sister, Mia, my brother, Ceejay, and to my in-laws, Carmelita and Erlin who have always been supportive, I am forever grateful.

To my daughter, Sammy—who has given me a new lens on life, has challenged me in the best way possible, you are the sweetest miracle and the strongest person I know. Thank you for teaching us so much about life and human behavior, every single day. You are limitless, unstoppable, and amazing. You inspire me. And to my husband, Erwin, who supports me and my dreams—no questions asked. You fill my heart. Your love is all I need.

To my pops in heaven, I hope I made you proud. I sprinkled a little bit of you in the *matchmaker*.

And to all my readers, there is something for everyone within these pages. May this book be some kind of escape...*some kind of remedy.*

Please leave a review on Amazon and Goodreads.
Share a picture of you and your copy of HEARTS and ERRORS
on social media. Share your favorite quotes from the book and tag
Corey M.P. @coreympwrites.
Use #heartsanderrorsanovel and #heartsanderrorsbycoreymp

Visit Corey's website for more information:
www.coreymp.com.

Twitter: coreympwrites
Instagram: coreympwrites
Facebook: coreympwrites

hearts and errors

BOOK CLUB QUESTIONS

1. What did you like best about HEARTS AND ERRORS?
2. How did you feel when the story ended?
3. What surprised you most about this book?
4. Did you enjoy the twists and turns within the story?
5. Which characters in the book did you like best, and why?
6. Can you relate to any of the characters? If so, who and why?
7. Did you reread any passages? Which ones?
8. Share a favorite quote from the book. Why did the quote stand out to you?

Here are a few to ponder on:

"I realize now that sometimes failed plans are disguised as missed opportunities but are meant to take us somewhere magical." (Lana Levine)

"Maybe sometimes, the best things in life are the things we can't explain and the things we can't understand. Maybe they don't make sense because they don't have to." (Lana Levine)

"Maybe that's why I wanted to get lost somewhere, because I wanted to be found." (Lana Levine)

9. What feelings did this book evoke for you?
10. Which scene stuck out to you the most, and why?
11. Lana's friendships are important to her. In the story, Cindy and Danielle face different stages of their lives. Do you think seeing what they were going through impacted Lana's life and relationship choices in any way?
12. If you were in Lana's shoes, is there anything you would have done differently during her challenges with her career and her relationships?
13. If you were making a movie of this book, who would you cast as Lana? Who would you cast as Jean-Luc?
14. Music is an important part of HEARTS AND ERRORS. Aside from "Wish You Were Here" by Pink Floyd and *"Parlez-moi d'amour"* by Lucienne Boyer, what other songs would you add to the playlist?
15. If you got the chance to ask the author of this book one question, what would it be?
16. Paris plays a huge role in Lana and Jean-Luc's love story. What's your favorite Paris scene or chapter?
17. What do you think of the book's title?

18. What do you think of the book's new edition cover?
19. How well do you think the author built the world in the book?
20. Did the characters seem believable to you? Did they remind you of anyone?
21. Did the book's pace seem too fast/too slow/just right?
22. If you were to write fanfic about this book, what kind of story would you want to tell?
23. What other books by Corey M.P. have you read?
24. Would you read another book by Corey M.P.?
25. Would you recommend this book to others?